Showdown

John laid his rifle aside and rose from his hiding place and started walking toward the road. His right hand rested on the butt of his pistol.

"Hobart," he called.

There was a loud grunt and Hobart stood up. His right hand was cocked like a frozen bird above his pistol.

"That you, Savage?" Hobart said.

"Looks like it's just you and me, Ollie," John said. "Isn't that the way you wanted it?"

"Damned right, Savage. You been breathin' my air too long."

Hobart's hand dove for his pistol as he went into a fighting crouch.

John stood straight, his right hand like magic as it jerked his pistol from its holster . . .

Berkley titles by Jory Sherman

THE VIGILANTE
THE VIGILANTE: SIX-GUN LAW
THE VIGILANTE: SANTA FE SHOWDOWN

THE DARK LAND
SUNSET RIDER
TEXAS DUST
BLOOD RIVER
THE SAVAGE GUN
THE SUNDOWN MAN
THE SAVAGE TRAIL
THE SAVAGE CURSE

The Savage Curse

Jory Sherman

BERKLEY BOOKS, NEW YORK

THE BERKLEY PUBLISHING GROUP
Published by the Penguin Group
Penguin Group (USA) Inc.
375 Hudson Street, New York, New York 10014, USA
Penguin Group (Canada), 90 Eglinton Avenue East, Suite 700, Toronto, Ontario M4P 2Y3, Canada
(a division of Pearson Penguin Canada Inc.)
Penguin Books Ltd., 80 Strand, London WC2R 0RL, England
Penguin Group Ireland, 25 St. Stephen's Green, Dublin 2, Ireland (a division of Penguin Books Ltd.)
Penguin Group (Australia), 250 Camberwell Road, Camberwell, Victoria 3124, Australia
(a division of Pearson Australia Group Pty. Ltd.)
Penguin Books India Pvt. Ltd., 11 Community Centre, Panchsheel Park, New Delhi—110 017, India
Penguin Group (NZ), 67 Apollo Drive, Rosedale, North Shore 0632, New Zealand
(a division of Pearson New Zealand Ltd.)
Penguin Books (South Africa) (Pty.) Ltd., 24 Sturdee Avenue, Rosebank, Johannesburg 2196,
South Africa

Penguin Books Ltd., Registered Offices: 80 Strand, London WC2R 0RL, England

This is a work of fiction. Names, characters, places, and incidents either are the product of the author's imagination or are used fictitiously, and any resemblance to actual persons, living or dead, business establishments, events, or locales is entirely coincidental.

THE SAVAGE CURSE

A Berkley Book / published by arrangement with the author

PRINTING HISTORY
Berkley edition / November 2008

ISBN: 978-0-425-22447-2

BERKLEY®
Berkley Books are published by The Berkley Publishing Group,
a division of Penguin Group (USA) Inc.,
375 Hudson Street, New York, New York 10014.
BERKLEY® is a registered trademark of Penguin Group (USA) Inc.
The "B" design is a trademark belonging to Penguin Group (USA) Inc.

PRINTED IN THE UNITED STATES OF AMERICA

10 9 8 7 6 5 4 3 2 1

For Brandon Jones
and his kung fu dog, Charlie

1

JOHN SAVAGE GAZED DOWN THE LONG TRAIL. THERE SEEMED NO
end to it, and its vacancy only added sting to the nettles of
worry that prickled in his mind. So many long trails, so much
empty space, bereft of all humanity, of succor to a troubled
man. Ben Russell, who rode alongside him, was no comfort
nor company. Ben was full of both advice and criticism and
he spouted them both with the regularity of a water clock.
When Ben was silent, John could still hear him ticking.

"You might think of stopping somewheres, John," Ben
said after nearly ten minutes of blessed silence. "That old
sun is headin' for the barn."

John looked up at the afternoon sky, saw the long loaves
of clouds floating in the western sky, their soft underbellies
tinged with peach and salmon, as if they were baking in a
blue oven. The sun hovered above the horizon, a boiling disk
of unrelenting heat, a magnet for sweat and flies, it seemed,
sucking out salt and water for the flies to feed on like diminu-
tive vultures at a watering hole.

"Soon as we find a water hole, Ben," Savage said. "Our
canteens have been dry a day and a half."

"Hell, look at it," Ben said. "Nary a cottonwood or a

shade tree. No people, neither. You picked a hell of a journey this time, John."

"I didn't pick it. Hobart did."

Oliver Hobart, the man responsible for murdering John's father, mother, sister, and a bunch of other miners in Colorado, was known to be headed for Tucson. John aimed to see that Tucson was Hobart's last refuge at the end of a long bloody trail.

"You just can't let it go, can you, John? Hell, we done killed most of the men who worked for Hobart. Ain't that enough for you?"

"No, Ben. Hobart's got to pay, too. Most of all, he's the one who has to pay."

John worried the small pebble in his mouth to stave off his thirst. He knew Ben was wallowing one just like it in his mouth. The horses were parched, too. They were starting to drag their hooves every now and then, and their sweat had dried, leaving dark patches of slick hide to shine in the sun, little granules of dried salt to glitter like crushed diamonds on their ribs and backsides.

John spat and no saliva came out of his mouth. He swallowed and nothing went down his throat beyond a fresh ache. The dryness made his throat sore and the air he drew in made his throat even dryer.

The land undulated and the old road dipped with its fall, and they would ride across old creek beds, or low places that showed signs of false floods where there was seldom any steady rain. Lakes shimmered ahead of them, only to vanish when they rode close, and the brightness played hob with a man's eyes. Both Ben and John squinted now at a mirage that danced a half mile in front of them, little tendrils of light streaming upward from it as if steaming in a morning mist. The phantom lakes could make a thirsty man go mad, John thought, but he hadn't felt a surge of hope after seeing his first one, a good long week ago.

"Supposed to be a well along here somewhere," John said. "Down in one of these bottoms."

"Last well we come across was plumb dried up," Ben said.

"Horses will smell it."

"You hope."

John said nothing. Ben was just in his usual argumentative mood and he knew he could not win against him. Ben had his ways. A man could get used to them, but he didn't have to tolerate them all the time. He knew he was probably wrong in going after Hobart over such desolate country, but he couldn't get the images of the slaughter at the mining camp out of his mind. Hobart and his men had ridden up without warning, shooting and yelling, killing everybody along the creek, showing no mercy. He and Ben had been up in a mine, looking down at them, helpless as sod. Neither of them had been armed and they knew if they ran down to help, they would have been shot down like all the rest.

Maybe the guilt he carried about that day was muddling his mind, but killing Hobart, making him pay for what he'd done, had become an uncontrollable obsession with him. And Hobart had gone on killing and robbing. The man was ruthless. He didn't deserve to live.

As they neared the top of the rise, John's horse, Gent, whickered low in his throat and his ears stiffened to hard cones, pitched forward.

"What is it, boy?" John said softly. "You smell water?"

He looked back at Ben's horse, Blaster. The roan was just plodding along, head drooping. But Gent had his head up and the trotter's step had quickened slightly.

John eased up on the reins, giving Gent his head. Gent, to his surprise, did not bolt, nor even increase his pace. Instead, the horse shied away from the top of the rise.

John took command, reined the horse hard, touched blunt spurs to his flanks. Gent broke into a trot, but to John he felt stiff and unwilling. Something wasn't right. Usually, Gent would break into a gallop at the prod of a spur in his flank, or at least jump into a trot. The horse was wary. Afraid of something.

But what?

"Come on, boy," John said to the horse and poked Gent's flanks with his spurs, digging in deeper than before.

Gent wrestled with the bit, took it in his teeth.

John felt his anger rise.

He jerked the reins, fought with Gent over control.

Gent started to turn back just as they topped the rise.

John loosened the reins, felt them go slack. Then, as Gent bowed his head and began to turn, John wrestled the bit from the horse's teeth, pulled hard, stopping Gent in mid-turn.

"What the hell's wrong with Gent?" Ben said.

"I don't know. Something's got him spooked."

"Well, he ain't sniffin' water, that's for sure."

Ben rode ahead, topped the rise. John saw the horse's rump drop below the rise, then stop. He heard a rustle of cloth, the snort of Ben's horse.

John rammed his spurs into Gent's flanks. The horse bucked ahead, topped the rise.

What he saw next brought a choking lump up into his throat, a queasy boil to his stomach.

Ben was stopped, both hands in the air. Off to the side, also on horseback, sat a man with a double-barreled shotgun leveled at Ben's head.

"You hold up there, Pilgrim," the man said.

John saw the man's thumb touch the crosshatched hammers of both barrels.

Click. Click.

Then the man swung the shotgun in John's direction.

John's blood turned ice cold in his veins.

He stared into the twin snouts of the shotgun.

Never had death been so close, he thought. So close.

Time seemed to hang up, smother all sound, all movement, all life in a single second of eternity.

He saw the man's index finger begin to curl around the front trigger. Just a slight movement that seemed so slow he almost missed it.

Out of the corner of his eye, down in the bottom, he saw a small wagon covered with a tarp, hitched to a mule. A man stood next to a pile of stones, buck naked, his clothes a puddle of cloth at his feet.

All that in a single instant.

And death hovered just above John's head like a hawk, suspended there for a thousand lifetimes compressed into that single electric minute.

The shotgunner's finger started to close on the front trigger.

2

THE MAN HOLDING THE SHOTGUN FINALLY SPOKE, JUST BEFORE HIS finger was about to touch the front trigger.

"Start shuckin' them clothes, gents," he said. "Take off them gunbelts first."

Ben lowered one arm. He pulled his hat off, tipping it to one side, then hurled it at the gunman, sailing it straight at his face. The shotgunner flinched and moved his head with an instinctive lean to avoid being hit.

John's right hand dropped like a diving hawk to the butt of his pistol. He drew it from its holster, thumbing back the hammer before it cleared leather. A split second later, the gun was level, pointed at the stranger, bucking with the explosion of the ignited powder.

All of this happened so fast, the man with the shotgun didn't even have time to cry out before the lead bullet smashed into his breastbone, just to the left of his heart. The projectile punched a hole through his chest, splintering bone as it flattened out into a deadly mushroom that smashed flesh, ripped out a piece of his heart, tore apart veins, crushed sinew and muscle as it sped through to the backbone, cracking it like a stick of wood. The bullet blew out his back, leaving a hole the size of a fifty-cent piece and spewing a rosy spray of blood outward in a misty fan.

The force of the bullet caved the man in, pushed him back against the cantle of his saddle. His fingers went limp and the shotgun tumbled from his hands, bounced on its butt as it struck the ground, teetered there on its wobbly axis for a moment, then fell over, hitting rocks with an iron clatter that sounded like a tumbler in a broken lock. The man opened his mouth to scream in that brief moment of pain. A fountain of blood gushed from his mouth, strangling him so that all that came out was a deathly gurgle. He crumpled and fell from his horse like a sack of meal, hitting the ground with a thud.

A pale blue snake of smoke twisted out of the barrel of John's pistol. His eyes glittered with a hot light as he stared at the fallen man. John's face was a mask, but his eyes reflected a mixture of anger and bewilderment.

"God," Ben breathed.

The word seemed to snap John out of his trance. He blew the smoke from his pistol into shreds and looked around as his thumb pressed down on the hammer and slowly drew the hammer back to full cock.

"He's the onliest one," Ben whispered.

"You sure?"

"That naked feller down there what was froze like a statue is a dancin' a jig, grinnin' like a shit-eatin' dog."

John looked down at the man who was hopping around in a circle, flapping his arms up and down, his dangle flopping like a beheaded snake.

"Damned idiot," Ben muttered.

John eased the hammer back down, slid the pistol back in its holster.

"What was the 'God' for, Ben?"

"I thought we was goners, John. You emptied his saddle pretty damned quick."

"You throwing your hat did the trick."

"That was a damned fool thing to do, now that I think on it."

Ben climbed down from his saddle and retrieved his hat.

He stepped around the dead man, eyeing him with a suspicious gander, his nose wrinkled as if he were smelling a pile of offal. He put his hat back on and walked back to his horse.

"Whooooeee," whooped the naked man. "You done saved my life, fellers."

John watched Ben pull himself back into the saddle.

"Well, we goin' down there, John, or are you going to just sit here and gloat?"

"I'm not gloating. I didn't want to kill that man."

"No, but I'm sure glad you did. He was ready to cut loose on us with both barrels of that Greener."

"Seems like," John said. "The bastard was ready to pull those triggers, all right."

"Damned road agents. Seems like you just can't get clear of 'em."

The naked stranger ran toward them as Ben and John rode down the slope. He was hollering and flapping his arms like some inmate who just escaped from an asylum.

"Lordy, I never seed such shootin'," the man declared. "Quick as lightning, that draw. Ooohhh, man oh man, I mean quick."

"Hold on, feller," John said as he rode up. "What's going on here?"

"You done saved my bare ass, Pilgrim, that's what's goin' on. I stopped at that well to get a drink and that jasper with the scattergun come out of nowhere, got the drop on me. Made me strip down so's he could rob me. For a minute there, I didn't know whether he was going to kill me or put the boots to me like I was some scarlet whore."

John looked around. There were low hills off to the right and some to the left where a man on horseback might hide, but no place of concealment real close.

"Those stones there," John said. "That's the water hole?"

"It's a danged well, all right. See that gully yonder? That robber come out of that."

The man pointed to a depression John hadn't noticed, a kind of gully that was overgrown with brush, a washout from some previous flood. It was difficult to see unless one was right on top of it. The gully lay about thirty yards from the well.

"I see it," John said. "Must be pretty deep."

"Deep enough to hide a man on horseback. Looks like an old mine pit, yes, sir, that's what it looks like, all right."

The man appeared to be in his late forties or early fifties. He was clean-shaven except for a drooping moustache streaked with blond hair that matched the long locks streaming down the back of the man's neck. He had a bald streak that parted his pate square in the middle. Crackling blue eyes, rheumy from strong drink or onion shavings. Gangly-legged and bony as a plucked crane, his skin was bone-white except for his neck and face, which were deep-tanned, dark as an elk's hide.

"I got to thank you, stranger, for putting that brigand down. They call me Peaches, 'cause I'm from Georgia, but my name's Pete Wainwright and that's my trade. I build and fix wagons for folks, yes, sir, from Tucson to Abilene and points south."

"Better get your duds back on," John said.

Ben kept his horse at a distance from Pete Wainwright as if the man were a loose cog in some rattletrap of a machine. The man jumped as he stepped with his bare feet on sharp and rounded stones. Instead of going back to put his clothes on, he clambered up the slope to where the dead man lay. He squatted down and began stripping the corpse of gunbelt and boots. He turned the pockets inside out, scooped up a handful of coins. He grabbed the man's hat and put it on. He gingerly hopped back down, carrying the shotgun and the gunbelt slung over his shoulders. He had slipped his bare feet into the dead man's boots.

"You want this stuff, mister?" Wainwright said. "They rightfully belong to you. I mean you kilt the man what owned them."

"No," John said. "You keep the stuff."

He swung out of the saddle and lifted the four empty canteens hanging from his saddle horn. He led Gent to the well where there was a crude wooden trough. He pulled the rope up, filled the trough with water. Then he filled his wooden canteens, set them down next to the well.

"I'll fill yours, Ben," he said. "Just hand them to me."

Wainwright stowed the shotgun, pistol, and gunbelt in his wagon, then slipped off the boots and threw those in, too. Then he slid into his long underwear and grabbed up his own shirt while John filled Ben's quartet of canteens. Gent and Blaster slurped water from the trough. Ben hauled the oaken bucket up and poured a little more water into the trough.

"Not too much," John said.

"I know. Don't want 'em to founder," Ben said. He drank from one of his canteens, wiped his lips. Both he and John walked around, stretching their tired legs. They had both been in the saddle since daybreak, following tracks that were days old, but still visible.

"I cut hair, too," Wainwright said after he was dressed. "You boys need haircuts, they'll be on me."

John stroked his beard. Usually clean-shaven, he hadn't bothered to scrape his face. He was intent on tracking Ollie Hobart and little else mattered to him.

"No, thanks," John said. "I can go a few more days before my beard turns on me."

"I carry one," Ben said. "Might trim it up when we get to Tucson."

"Headed for Tucson, are ye?" Wainwright said. "Dirty little town, full of rascals and thieves, like that one up yonder."

He inclined his head toward the corpse lying up the slope several yards away.

"I'm just looking for one thief," John said.

"He stole something from you, did he?"

"He stole just about everything from me."

"You don't want to join up with him, then?" Wainwright said.

Ben snorted.

"Hell no, friend. He wants to lay him out like he did that'un yonder." Ben cocked a thumb toward the dead man.

"Tucson ain't a big town," Wainwright said. "Maybe I

know where you can find this man. Owlhoots tend to stick
together."

"You talking about an outlaw hangout?" John said.

Wainwright laughed.

"They ain't no outlaws in Tucson," he said.

"No outlaws in Tucson?" Ben said. "I find that right hard
to believe."

"You got to have laws to have outlaws, mister," Wainwright said. "They ain't no law in Tucson. None to speak of
anyways."

"This man hasn't been there very long," John said. "You
probably wouldn't know him from Adam's off ox."

"This man got a name?"

"Hobart," John said, the word coming out of his mouth
like an oath, or a chunk of ripped flesh.

Wainwright's eyes went wide.

"Ollie Hobart?" Wainwright said, so soft John and Ben
could barely hear it.

"You know Ollie Hobart?" John said, his eyes aglitter
with a piercing light that seemed to come from within.

"Hell, he's the reason I left Tucson yesterday mornin',"
Wainwright said. "I don't know him. I know who he is. I
know his damned name."

"And how come you know him?" John said.

Wainwright dropped his head. He gurgled as if something was caught in his throat. When he looked back up at
John, his eyes were rimmed with tears. A single droplet hung
on the rim of his cheekbone.

"I didn't work alone," Wainwright said. "My son, Tim,
was my helper. Hobart shot him dead night before last. Shot
him dead right before my eyes, and for no good reason."

Ben and John exchanged looks.

"Hobart don't need no reason to kill anybody," Ben said.
"Ain't that right, John?"

John did not answer. He stood, staring at the grieving
man. Wainwright's eyes told it all. They were wet with tears
and more were flowing down his cheeks. He looked like a
lost soul, a man without a friend in the world when he most

needed one. It made John's stomach turn to know that Ollie Hobart was still doing what he always did, killing innocent people. He felt sorry for Wainwright.

He had long ago stopped feeling sorry for himself.

3

JOHN WALKED OVER TO A LARGE ROCK AND SAT DOWN. WAIN-
wright followed him and stood nearby as John took out his
pistol, thumbed the hammer back to half cock, opened the
gate to the cylinder, and ejected the empty brass hull. He
pushed a fresh bullet from his belt and slid it into the empty
spot, spun the cylinder, and closed the gate.

"You keep six in there?" Wainwright asked.

"Yes."

"Most don't. Safer to keep the hammer down on an empty
cylinder."

"Sometimes I need six."

"That's really a pretty six-gun you have there. Looks like
a Colt."

"It is, but my pa built it for me, filed down the sear, put
new parts in. Had it engraved."

"So I see. Inlaid silver, ain't it?"

John nodded.

"What's that say on the barrel there?"

"It's a Spanish saying," John said. *"No me saques sin razón, ni me guardes sin honor."*

"You speak Spanish real good. What's it mean, anyways?"

"Don't draw me without reason, nor keep me without honor."

"I reckon you abide by that," Wainwright said.

"He does," Ben said. "And you sure ask a lot of questions. You bury your boy in Tucson?"

"Yeah, right after that buzzard Hobart kilt him. I got out of Tucson real quick, too."

"How come?" Ben asked.

"Hobart let it be known that I might be next. He took a dislike to my boy Tim, and maybe he didn't like me much, either."

"Just like that?" John asked. "He shot your son for no reason?"

"Well, not exactly. Seems like Tim was sparking a gal there when Hobart come to town. Turns out that the gal was sweet on Hobart, and vice versa. Hobart didn't like competition. He told Tim to light a shuck when he walked in on the gal and Tim stood up to him."

Tears began to wet Wainwright's eyes again, and he stopped talking.

"I'm sorry," John said. "What was the gal's name? You know?"

"Diane Meacham. Hell, she never mentioned Hobart. But she knowed him before, I reckon. She works at a cantina there. It's got a pretty bad reputation. Seems like all the owlhoots wet their whistles in there."

"Why did Tim go there?" Ben asked.

"He was makin' a saddle for the owner, feller named Ortiz. Benito Ortiz. He finished the saddle, but plumb fell for Diane. Hell, he was just a kid. Barely nineteen. Diane's some older, maybe twenty-six or so."

"What's the name of that cantina?" John asked.

"La Copa. You can't miss it. Got a big old cup outside, up on the adobe roof. It's a pretty rough place. Knife fights, gunfights, fistfights, kick fights."

"No police?" Ben asked.

"Naw. None of 'em would go there, even if they was dyin' of thirst."

"How can I find it?" John asked.

"It's on a street named Alameda. Little street, more like an alley. Next to a blacksmith's we done some work for, man name of Rudolfo Alicante runs it. I built a cart for one of his customers."

"Thanks," John said and holstered his pistol. He stood up. "We'll be going on then, Mr. Wainwright. Where are you bound?"

"Headin' for Lordsburg."

"We came through Lordsburg," Ben said. "Ain't much there to brag about."

"Nope," Wainwright said. "But wagons to fix and build."

"You take care, Wainwright," John said.

"No, you take care, Mr. Savage. That Hobart's got a heap of friends in Tucson. Most of 'em put their boots on the rail at La Copa."

"I'll be careful," John said.

Ben snorted as if he knew better. Which he did.

John and Ben mounted up after hanging their canteens from their saddle horns and left Wainwright at the well. He waved to them and they waved back.

They topped the rise and saw Wainwright no more that afternoon.

"We might best be lookin' for a place to bed down for the night," Ben said after the sun had dropped another three fingers in the western sky. "I measure only two fingers left of sunlight."

When the sun was setting, a man could hold up the flat of his hand to the horizon, just below the sun, and count fifteen minutes for each finger. They had about thirty minutes before the sun set.

"I'm wondering where that drygulcher came from," John said. "He was waiting for Wainwright, according to him."

"That's right, he sure was," Ben said. "Like he knowed Wainwright would be along."

"Might be an owlhoot camp hereabouts."

"A godforsaken place, you ask me."

"If there is such a camp, it wouldn't be far from that well."

John scanned the ground for tracks that stood out from ones they already knew. There were tracks from Wainwright's cart and his mules, and tracks heading toward Tucson. The man he'd shot had left no tracks around the well, so he must have ridden straight to that little hideout to wait for Wainwright.

"Johnny, what are you thinkin'?"

"I'm thinking we ought to ride back a ways and backtrack that drygulcher's horse. See where he came from."

"Why? We ought to just keep ridin' toward Tucson, like we was doin', and leave well enough alone. You done killed one man today. Ain't that enough for you?"

"I just don't want to throw down my bedroll and have somebody sneak up on us in the dark. Didn't you ever hear that old expression 'Birds of a feather flock together'?"

"Meanin' in this case?"

"Meaning that jasper didn't just come from nowhere to way out here."

"He probably follered Wainwright all the way from Tucson."

"Followed him? Then why was he waiting in ambush for Wainwright? No, that boy spotted Wainwright and kept it to himself. He rode up there to that well and waited for him. He wasn't about to share his information with his cronies. And you can bet good money, his outlaw friends are not very far away."

"Johnny, we don't need no more trouble."

"Ben, I agree with you. We sure don't need any more trouble. But sometimes you have to listen to what you can't hear."

"Huh? That don't make no sense."

"I mean you have to pay attention to your instincts. That little voice up in your head that says, 'wait, look around, think.'"

"Yeah, I do that."

"Well, I'm hearing it now. You know, sometimes you can be all by yourself out in the middle of nowhere and you know, without seeing anybody, that you're not alone."

"I've had that happen sometimes. Not exactly like that, but maybe in a saloon, you feel like somebody's watchin' you and you turn around real quick and see somebody just a-starin' at you. Makes the hairs on my neck rise up and get stiff as hog bristles."

"Same feeling, Ben. Like the one I have now."

"You mean, like somebody's a-watchin' us right now?"

"Sort of. Like we're not alone out here. I got a feeling. Real strong."

"Well, I don't feel much like ridin' back to that well to scout for tracks."

"We don't have to, Ben. We'll leave this road and make a circle, see if we can pick up some tracks. If we do, we'll follow them back to where that feller came from. Likely, we'll find a hill or a mesa, maybe a small butte where that bushwhacker got a gander at Wainwright."

"Wild-goose chase if you ask me."

"Sometimes you catch the wild goose," Savage said. "Makes for a mighty fine meal."

Ben let out a mirthless laugh, dry as a sun-seared corn husk.

"You ain't goin' to listen to me, Johnny. You never do."

"I listen, Ben."

"Goes in one ear, out the other."

"Let's get off this road and see if we can find those tracks before dark." John turned Gent off the old wagon trail and rode off toward the north. Ben followed. Chamisa sage, ocotillo, rocks, and prickly pear dotted the desolate landscape. Not far away, the skyline was broken by small mesas, low buttes, rocky outcroppings where flash floods had piled up stones upon stones. John scanned the ground, looking for horse tracks.

Ben kept his gaze upon the surrounding country, looking for nothing in particular, but for anything that might catch his eye, stir his interest.

A jackrabbit bolted from cover, scampering more than a dozen yards. Then froze into rigid invisibility. The sun dropped lower in the sky and the distant clouds began to take on color, turning from snow white to pale salmon and peach. Some began to turn to a dusky purple and John knew he would not have much light left to track. He began to turn Gent into a wide circular path, arcing toward the west.

Then he saw disturbed ground.

He reined up Gent and studied the markings more closely, as if to unlock the secrets of desert travel.

"You got something, John?" Ben asked.

"I think we just struck that bushwhacker's trail, Ben. Can you make out those scuffs in the dirt?"

"I don't see nothin'," Ben said, squinting to focus his vision, magnify the ground where John was pointing.

John leaned over and guided Gent alongside the disturbed soil. He saw no clear track at first, just upturned dirt, stones that had been overturned, kicked away from their resting places to leave small smooth divots where they had been.

Ben was still squinting and seeing very little.

John saw a clear horseshoe track, very distinct. He rode on, following the open end of the horseshoe's direction. There was another track on an open patch of ground. He now knew the general direction of the rider who had left those tracks. He looked up, scanned the terrain from right to left, clear to the road.

Then he saw it, and his heart seemed to leap in his chest.

Near the road, less than a quarter mile away, there was a small butte, or what appeared to be a ridge rising above the flat land, like a sailing ship without a mast.

"Ben, look," John said. "That could be where the bushwhacker waited until he saw a likely citizen come down the road. Tracks lead right in back of that butte or mesa. He could see a long way from on top and have plenty of time to get on his horse and ride to the well."

"I see it," Ben said.

"Let's take a look," John said.

Ben held up four fingers to the horizon. Two of them filled the gap between the land and the sun.

"Be dark in about a half hour, Johnny. We might want to—"

John saw a flash of orange, then heard the crack of a rifle. He ducked and heard the sizzle of a bullet as it split the air over his head.

"Take cover, Ben," he shouted and rode for a nearby gully.

That shot had come from atop the butte. Two seconds later another shot rang out and the flash this time was from a place just below the butte, just an orange flower, then a blossom of white smoke. The bullet plowed a furrow between Gent's fore and rear legs. Gent bolted for the gully.

The horse scrambled down into rocks and brush. Ben came down into the depression at a gallop as another shot sounded and they both heard the whine of the bullet as it caromed off a rock.

John drew his rifle from its sheath and jumped from the saddle.

Ben dismounted with his rifle in hand, too.

"We're trapped like rats down here," Ben muttered. "They got us cold."

John said nothing.

Whoever was shooting at them was at least a quarter mile away. That gave him time to think and to look around.

The gulley looked like an old washout. Soft sand and rock, some brush. A lizard lay sprawled on a stone, yellow eyes staring at him, tail and body perfectly still.

John wasn't going to say it, but he thought they had only a few seconds to set up some kind of defense.

Otherwise, whoever rode up on them would find easy pickings.

It would be, he thought, like shooting fish in a barrel.

4

JOHN SCANNED THE BANK FACING THE BUTTE, LOOKING FOR A DE-
fensive position that would allow him to return fire. Water
and wind had cut a straight line down some of the wall, but
he found a spot where he might lean against it and bring his
rifle to bear on their attackers.

He stepped on a large rock for purchase, then slowly
raised his rifle and eased it over the edge of the gully. He
lifted his head until he could see down the barrel. He looked
for the two men he had seen shooting at them. The one on
top of the butte was gone. The one at the foot of the bluff
had also vanished. He heard the muffled sounds of hoofbeats fading away.

Ben scrambled up beside him.

"What do you make of it, Johnny?"

"They lit a shuck. That's odd."

"Mighty odd. What do you think?"

"Could be a trick. Or they could have lost heart."

"Why in hell did they shoot at us in the first place?"

"Beats me. But that's probably where that other jasper
spotted Wainwright and then took off to ambush him."

"You think so?"

"It's the highest point close to the road hereabouts."

The hoofbeats no longer sounded. It grew quiet as the two men leaned against the bank, their rifles resting on the flat ground. Somewhere in the distance, a quail piped a plaintive call and then that sound left a vacuum of silence that was almost deafening.

Then John heard a sound behind him that sent shivers up his spine, electric ripples that set every nerve in his body to tingling as if touched by icy fingers. A boot crunching on sand and gravel, followed by the *snick* of a cocking hammer. Ben heard it, too, and froze into a stiffened statue. John slowly turned his head and looked up. There, on the opposite bank, stood a man with a rifle pointed directly at him. A split second later, another man came into view and stood beside the first man. He cocked his rifle and aimed it at John.

"Well, well," the first man said, "look what we got here, Jesse."

"Yeah, a coupla drygulchers."

"Standin' in a dry gulch."

Both men laughed.

"Don't tech them rifles, boys," the second man said. "And better heist them hands in the air."

Ben and John lifted their hands in surrender.

"They got us cold, Johnny."

"And shet yore trap, old-timer," the first man said.

The second man looked toward the butte and gestured, motioning to someone to come his way. John heard hoofbeats a few moments later. The two men waited. The first man was chewing on a cud of tobacco and he spat into the dirt once, sending a stream of brown juice through his stained lips. The men both had five-day beards and neither had seen a barber in some time. They both had long hair streaming from under their hats.

Two riders rode up and John assumed that they were the men who had shot at them. Both brandished rifles. They sat their horses a little behind the other two men and looked down at John and Ben with lifeless brown eyes. They each shoved their rifles into their scabbards.

"Looks like you got you two owlhoots, Cruddy," the man on the buckskin said.

"How you figger that?" Cruddy said. His name was Billy Crudder, but everyone called him Cruddy.

"Look at 'em. Neither one has stood up close to a razor and they got so much dust on 'em they look like they been a-wallerin' in it."

"You boys on the owlhoot trail?" Cruddy asked.

Ben looked at John.

"Maybe," John said, his mind churning for time to think. "Depends on who's asking?"

"I'm askin'. And what you answer might make a difference."

"You the law?" John said, affecting an air of innocence. He put a little quaver in his voice to heighten the illusion he was trying to create.

Cruddy guffawed. The other three men laughed, too, with all the loudness of a churlish chorus in their cups.

"Do we look like the law?" Cruddy said.

John shrugged. Ben's face took on a puzzled blankness, but he said nothing.

"I—I don't know. Maybe. We were sure chased by a posse back there." He twitched a pointing finger to the east, behind where the four men stood.

"Lordsburg?"

"Yeah," John said, his voice dipping low into a disappointed growl.

Cruddy and the other gunmen exchanged knowing glances.

"You must be green as baby shit to try and pull off something in Lordsburg. Might as well poke a stick into a hornet's nest."

"Well, that's what we done," John said, warming to his lie. "Stuck up a pilgrim and had to light a shuck. Posse chased us clear across New Mexico."

The four men all guffawed with raucous gusto. Cruddy slapped a hand on his heisted leg and the two men on horseback doubled over in mirth.

The man standing next to Cruddy squeezed his eyes shut to block the tears. He was a thin razor of a man with long straggly hair and a grease-stained hat that looked as if it had been kicked over a hundred miles of rough country. His vest bore the faded colors of spilled grub and grog, and his boots were as scuffed as his splotchy face.

John stood there with that pasty look of dumbness that made his spurious account of banditry all the more ludicrous.

The rider at the end of the line of four was a stocky, grizzled man in his forties, with dark curly hair that tumbled from under his hat like curls of thin-shaved ebony. He had a cheroot sticking out from pudgy lips, small black eyes that were deep sunk behind high cheekbones. He looked slightly Oriental, but John thought he might be a half-breed. He was taciturn except when he laughed, and his laughter was on the scornful side, more reserved than the laughter of the others.

"Just who in hell did you boys rob?" Cruddy asked.

The thoughts whirled through John's mind like corks in a millrace.

"Turned out to be a preacher and his wife," John said, snatching up the first thought that bobbed up.

More guffaws. Except for the breed, who allowed John only a condescending sneer and a slight chuckle.

"A preacher?"

"That's what got the town all riled up," John said. "Hell, I didn't see that he was totin' a Bible. I thought it was a box of jewelry, or maybe cash."

Cruddy doubled over in laughter then. All but the breed laughed with him.

The shadows grew long as the sun descended into the mountain-edged sky. The gunmen seemed to be in no hurry, but bound to make sport with their captives before killing and robbing them. John had no doubt he could pull his pistol and drop at least one or two of the men up on the bank, but he didn't know if Ben could react fast enough to protect himself. He decided he'd better not risk it. Just play out the hand, he thought. At least the drygulchers seemed to be amused at his playacting. Maybe their sense of humor would prevail over their killer instincts. It was a long shot, but so far, none of the men had cocked a hammer or squeezed a trigger.

"You ever hear anything like that, Jubal?" Cruddy asked the man next to him.

"Dumber'n a sack full of rocks," Jubal said.

The men all chuckled.

John's palms began to sweat. He wanted his pistol in his hand so bad, he had to force himself to smile back at the men up on the bank. The two horses switched their tails and swatted at flies. One of them pawed the ground, impatient to get away from the darkening gully.

Ben crinkled his nose, trying to relieve an itch without using his hand. He shifted the weight on his feet as one of them began to grow numb.

"You better get serious, Cruddy," the breed said. He was sitting on a steeldust gray with cropped mane.

"Hell, Horky, I was just havin' a little fun."

"Well, ask them if they seen Bud. He warn't nowhere up on that mesa. Just his tracks." This from the man on the buckskin, the one called Jubal.

"I was getting to that. But . . ."

John was trying to figure out who the leader of the bunch was. He couldn't tell from the way they acted. Cruddy did all the talking. The breed didn't say much, the one called Horky, and Jubal hadn't taken charge. He was just watching, like the others.

"But what?" Jubal said.

"I got a better question to ask."

"Well, go ahead and ask it then," Jubal said.

"You boys got any money? Any greenbacks, silver, or gold?"

"A little," John said. "We were running short in Lordsburg and thought we'd pick up some cash. If it wasn't for bad luck back there, we would have had no luck at all. We're pretty broke."

John hoped he sounded convincing. He could almost hear Ben groan inwardly at the lies he was spewing. But he knew

Ben was smart enough not to say a word. His arms were getting tired, holding them up like that. He wished one of the men holding guns on them would make some kind of move. Give him an excuse to go for his pistol. It would probably be the last thing he'd ever do, he thought.

Then, to his surprise, Ben spoke.

"We ain't et in two, three days," Ben said.

John could have kissed him.

With those words, Ben had probably saved both their lives.

5

SHADOWS BEGAN TO CRAWL UP THE EAST SIDE OF THE GULLY.

"You boys want something to eat?" Cruddy said. "Maybe get acquainted?"

"That would be better than standing here like a couple of scarecrows," John said.

"We might have somethin' in common," Cruddy said. "What do you think, Jubal?"

"It's okay by me, Cruddy."

"Horky?"

"I could use some grub myself."

"Maybe we better lighten them up some before we let 'em ride with us," the other man said, the quiet one on the buckskin.

"Yeah," Cruddy said. "Set your rifles up here on the bank and unbuckle your gunbelts. Just until we know you better."

John hesitated. It could be a trick, he thought. If he let himself and Ben be disarmed, they wouldn't have a chance against four men.

"Sure, we can do that," Ben said, surprising John. "Hunger is a mighty powerful coax."

"Hear that, Jubal? A mighty powerful coax. Mister, you got a gift of gab."

Ben smiled wanly, as if he had been punched in the stomach. John glanced at him, but Ben was already turning around, reaching for his rifle.

John got his rifle and carried it to the bank, lay it alongside Ben's. Ben unbuckled his gunbelt, wrapped it into a wad of leather and cartridges, and set it alongside his rifle. John shrugged and did the same.

"Lead your horses on up here," Cruddy said. "Jubal, you collect their hardware and pass some to Horky and Dan."

John's blood began to boil, but he held his temper as he and Ben walked out of the gully. The leaves on the paloverde trees were losing their color in the twilight and the saguaros stood like silent sentinels as far as the eye could see, broken only by the rising hills with varied geometrical shapes, mesas, spires, cones, flatirons, and buttes. The land took on a mystical quality at that time of day, and such a hush that he could hear his own breathing, the thumping pump of his heart as he climbed onto the flat.

"You boys can mount up. Just foller us."

John turned to his horse and climbed into the saddle. He avoided looking at Ben. Ben could read him too well, even if he kept that blank look on his face. He wanted to strangle Cruddy and was still berating himself for giving up his rifle and pistol.

He felt naked and vulnerable as he and Ben followed the men. They were prisoners without shackles, disarmed, helpless, and outnumbered.

Crudder led the procession, which had fallen into a semblance of a military unit with lead rider, flankers, and the halfbreed riding drag. They turned right before they reached the butte and entered what appeared to be a narrow defile between two low hills dotted with ocotillo, prickly pear, and cholla. Then Crudder turned right again and they entered a highwalled canyon that was now dark as the sun disappeared. The trail wound through the canyon and twisted through smaller canyons, until it seemed to John that they were in the midst of a puzzling maze.

"We'll never find our way back through this," Ben whispered to John. "If they let us go, or if we escape."

"It does not look good," John admitted.

Finally, Crudder took a left-hand turn through an opening in the canyon wall and the riders entered it. The fissure narrowed until they were all riding single file through almost total darkness.

The narrow passage led to an open place that appeared to be enclosed by walls. In the gloom, John made out a number of adobe dwellings, each tucked against a canyon wall, each in shadow. They almost looked like illusions, just faint impressions of doors and windows. The silence was intense until he heard the wind whistling over them, brushing past the high walls in a heavy whisper.

A fire glimmered in one of the adobe huts. Crudder headed for it. A man stepped out, leveling a rifle at him.

"That you, Cruddy?"

"Yeah, Jake."

"You gained a man or two."

"Two. We run acrost a pair of owlhooters."

"Well, come on in. They's beans in the pot and a chunk of beef floatin' on the bottom."

John looked around for other horses, but didn't see any. Crudder dismounted and walked up to the man he had called Jake. He handed the reins of his horse to Jake and then beckoned to John to dismount.

"This here's Jake Ward. He'll put up your horse."

Ward took the reins from John, handed them to Horky. John looked at Ward a long time, watched the way he walked. Something about him seemed familiar.

"I didn't get your name, I reckon," Crudder said, breaking into John's thoughts. John thought quickly.

"Logan. Johnny Logan," he said quickly.

"Well, Johnny, likely we'll get to know each other better after we all have some vittles and some hot coffee after supper. Gets mighty chilly out here in the desert at night."

"I know," John said.

Horky and the others dismounted, along with Ben. Horky took Ben's horse and followed Jake to a fissure in the canyon wall behind the firelit adobe. The horses and men disappeared as John stood next to Crudder.

"Yeah, we got a big ol' corral back there with several head of beef. Makes a good hideout, wouldn't you say?"

"What is this place?" John asked.

"I think Yaqui used this place to hide from the army. Some say it was built by Navajo or some such tribe, maybe the Havasupai. Lots of legends in this country."

John felt a queasiness in his stomach. He could no longer hear either the horses or the men. It was as if they had been swallowed up by this secret canyon. The quiet was so thick, he thought he could cut it with a knife. The roiling in his stomach he recognized as something close to fear. He and Ben were completely at the mercy of these outlaws. Crudder held all the cards and owned the deck.

"Jake," Crudder said, "I didn't give you this feller's handle a while ago. Goes by the name of Johnny Logan."

"Logan," Ward said, avoiding John's penetrating gaze. "I better see to the fire."

Ward went inside the adobe. John could see his silhouette against the blazing light of the fire. John's brows knitted in thought, but all the thoughts were dead ends, leading nowhere.

Ben came back, walking with Horky. The others followed. All except Ben were smoking cigarettes. The tips glowed in the gathering gloom like fireflies on a summer night. The smoke hung in the still air like morning steam along a river.

"Horky here," Ben said to John, "used to herd sheep up in Colorado. When he was a kid. Small world, eh, Johnny?"

John flashed Ben a look, shook his head slightly.

Ben caught on fast and shut up.

The men went inside the adobe. The cook fire made it hot inside, but when John leaned against a wall, the adobe was cool. He studied the faces of the men as they squatted around the room, their faces lit by firelight. When Hobart and his gang had murdered his parents and the other prospectors in

Colorado, he had memorized all their faces. He wanted to be sure that none of these men had been there that day, that none had been in Hobart's bunch. He recognized none of them, but his gaze lingered on Ward longer than on the others.

"Well, boys," Crudder said, hefting Ben's gunbelt, which was still wrapped up in a bundle of leather, bullets, and buckle. "Shall we trust these owlhoots with their weapons?"

"If you vouch for 'em, Cruddy," Ward said. "They look all right to me."

"Um, I do not know," Horky said. "We do not know nothing about them."

"They ain't wearin' badges," Jubal Mead said. "That's good enough for me."

"We ain't gonna vote, are we?" Jesse said. "I can't tell who a man is just by lookin' at him."

Crudder turned to look at John Savage.

"You want to join up with us, Logan?" he said.

"Depends," John said. "We don't know much about outlawin'."

Crudder and the others laughed. All but Ward, who narrowed his eyes as he gazed at Savage.

"That's for sure," Crudder said, and then he told Ward about the Logans robbing a preacher in Lordsburg. "They may be dumb, but at least they tried."

Horky picked up John's gunbelt and unwrapped it. He slid the pistol from its holster and let out a long low whistle.

"That is a pretty six-gun," he said. He bent his head and held the engraved inscription up to the firelight and mouthed the words inscribed on the barrel in silver inlay.

"No me saques sin razón, ni me guardes sin honor," he read.

"What's that gibberish, Horky?" Crudder asked.

"It's Spanish," Jubal said. "Don't you know nothin', Cruddy?"

"What's he doin' with a Spanish pistol?" Cruddy asked.

"My father gave it to me," John said.

"I know what it says," Ward said. "I speak a little of the lingo."

"Well, spit it out," Crudder said.

"I'll save him the trouble," John said. "It says, 'Don't draw me without reason, nor keep me without honor.'"

"It sure is a purty pistol," Crudder said, taking it from Horky. "Looks like a Colt .45."

"It started out that way," John said. "My daddy modified it, engraved it, inlaid it with silver. I'd like to have it back. It means a lot to me."

Crudder squinted as he turned the pistol over in his hands.

"Might trade you for it," he said.

John fought to keep his emotions from showing on his face. All of the outlaws looked at him. Crudder had made an offer.

John Savage's life depended, he thought, on his answer.

Ward cleared his throat. Ben looked as if he had been kicked in the stomach.

The fire crackled and the water in the pot came to a rolling boil. Steam rose into the air and the room felt as hot as a sweatbox.

Nobody moved.

Waiting for John's answer.

6

HORKY STEPPED INTO THE CONVERSATION BEFORE JOHN COULD reply to Crudder.

"That gun has a curse on it," he said.

"Huh?" Crudder looked over a Horcasitas.

"What it says on the barrel. That is a curse. If you break its promise, that gun will kill you."

Crudder looked down at the pistol, then at John.

"What's he talkin' about, Logan?" he asked.

Savage felt the intensity of every man in the room. They all had their gaze fixed on him. Even Ben, who seemed to be holding his breath.

"It is a kind of curse," John said, speaking slowly, as if measuring every word. "My daddy said it meant bad luck if I broke that vow he etched onto the barrel of that pistol. He said he put it there to keep me from being hotheaded. He wanted me to think twice before I took a man's life. I guess it was good advice . . ." John's voice trailed off into a softness of tone that gripped every man in the room. Including Ben.

"Wh—what the hell you getting at, Logan?" Crudder asked.

"My—my pa, he—he shot a man with that pistol before

he gave it to me . . ." Again, John left his words floating, the sentence seemingly unfinished.

"And what happened to your pa?" Crudder asked, his voice a strangled croak issuing from his throat.

"Right after he shot a man to death, Pa's horse threw him. Pa broke his neck."

"Aw, that don't mean nothin'," Crudder said. But there was a quaver in his voice, like a man whistling in the dark when he passes a cemetery.

"Maybe," John said, fixing Crudder with a hard gaze. "But Pa's gunbelt was dangling from his saddle horn at the time. Pa's foot got tangled in the stirrup. The horse bucked and the gunbelt looped around my pa's neck. Then the horse dragged him through a mile of brush and the gunbelt caught on a rock and snapped my pa's neck. When we found him, that gunbelt looked like a noose around his neck and the pistol was right under his jaw." John paused to let his words sink in. There wasn't so much as a breath in the room. "Just like a hangman's knot."

Crudder swore and the gunbelt turned hot in his hands. He looked down at it as if he held a poisonous snake in his hands. Then he lifted the rig with both hands and hurled the bundle at John, who caught it.

"Keep your damned gun, Logan," Crudder said.

Ward's eyes narrowed as he looked at Savage. His lips arced in a faint curve that resembled a knowing smile.

Jubal Mead broke the silence.

"Let's get at them vittles," he said. "I'm so hungry I could eat the south end of a northbound horse."

Horky belched out a nervous laugh.

"Hell, let's eat," Ward said, and the tension in the room subsided.

Horky tossed Ben's gunbelt to him as he rose to his feet. Ben caught it. He wore a surprised look on his face. The look vanished as he strapped on the rig, adjusting the holster so that it nestled like a cup in a saucer to his leg.

"They's bowls aplenty here," Cruddy said. "Help yourselves. Horky, get us some spoons, will you?"

The men ate while Crudder explained to John and Ben about the spring that fed a well, giving them an abundance of sweet water. They had found eating utensils in every hogan and ollas filled with corn and flour.

"It was like all the people here left in the middle of the night," he said. "Just packed up and left, leavin' behind blankets and goods. We didn't find this place, but we heard about it. Some waddy stumbled into this maze of canyons by accident and marked his trail when he come out. It sounded like a good hideout, so we come here a few days ago."

"It appears to have everything you need," John said. "Were you chased here?"

Crudder laughed.

"We was chased, all right. Couple of men wearin' stars on their chests and a pack of trigger-happy galoots they rounded up in a Tucson cantina. None of 'em had the brains of a pissant."

The other outlaws laughed.

"They were Injuns," Ward explained. "Superstitious. We heard later that they refused to follow our tracks in here. Run off and left the deputies scared of their own shadows."

More laughter.

John was beginning to get a picture of the outlaws, but it was sketchy, murky, like trying to find color in a pan full of mud. He was interested, though, because he wondered about men like Hobart who chose a life of crime instead of pursuing legal means to earn money. These men seemed content with their lot in life, but it was a rootless, restless life that offered few rewards in the long run. He wondered why they had chosen to become outlaws. He wondered why Hobart was such a cold-blooded killer. The puzzle was too enormous to comprehend or unravel that night, but he was bound to learn all he could about these men and, at the first opportunity, to get as far away from them as possible. He was sure that Ben felt the same. For now, however, they both had to play along with Crudder and his bunch, or their lives might not be worth a plugged nickel.

When the meal was over, they all scraped their bowls with

dirt and Horky rinsed them and their spoons, then stacked them on a flat stone next to a wall. The men all walked outside to smoke and look at the stars. Ward stayed behind, telling Crudder he'd be along in a while.

"You don't smoke, Logan?" Ward said to John.

"No. I never picked up the habit."

"Ben?"

"I smoke a pipe now and again," Ben said.

Then Ward did a curious thing. He stepped close to John and whispered in his ear.

"I know who you are, John Savage."

Ben just barely heard the name "Savage" and walked over, his knees quivering as if they were filled with jelly.

John stiffened, but his expression did not change.

"You must be mistaken," he said.

"Look at me, John. Don't you recognize who I am?"

John studied Ward's face. There was something vaguely familiar about it. But he did not recognize the man as someone he knew. He shook his head.

"I'm sorry," John said. "I don't know you."

"Don't I look familiar to you?"

"A little," John admitted.

"I never met you, but I heard my brother talk about you. He mentioned your name in a couple of his letters. That is, if your pa was Dan Savage. And, your ma, she was named Clare. And you had a little sister named Alice. Just a tadpole, my brother said."

Ben swore under his breath. A light of recognition flashed in his eyes. He slapped his knee and let out a long breath.

"You're Jesse Ward's kid brother, ain't you?" Ben said.

Before he answered, John knew who he was.

"Sure," John said. "Jake Ward. Jesse told us about you. He was mighty proud of you, in fact. What happened to you? How come you're an owlhooter?"

"Hell, John, I think we're both after the same man," Ward said.

"What?"

"Hobart. When I got news of what happened up at your

diggings, I took off on a week's drunk. Then I rode out to
Denver, took up in Cherry Creek, and started hearing stories
about you hunting down the men who killed your family.
And my brother Jesse. I been huntin' Hobart ever since.
These boys here think I'm just like them, but I ain't."

"You mean you're just playactin'?" Ben said.

Ward grinned sheepishly.

"Never thought of it that way, but sort of, I reckon. I
threw in with these jaspers and I've learned a lot."

"They in with Hobart?" John asked.

Ward smiled.

"No time to get into that now. They'll get suspicious if I
don't go out there and chew the fat with 'em. 'Sides, I need a
smoke. You two just sit tight. We can talk in the mornin'
maybe."

Ward left before John could ask him another question. He
scrunched up his face in disappointment.

"I can see it now," Ben said, his voice still pitched to a
low whisper.

"What?"

"His resemblance to Jesse. Jake's a younger copy of his
brother."

"Jesse always scraped his face every morning. Jake's got
a three-day beard. That threw me off."

"You reckon we're going to get out of here alive? Hell, I
couldn't find my way back out if my life depended on it."

"The way it looks, if Jake plays it straight with us, we'll
ride out with Crudder and the others. Maybe he'll lead us
right to Hobart."

Ben sucked in a breath, held it for a moment, then let out
a long sigh.

"A lot of ifs, you ask me."

"We have no choice, Ben. We're in the pickle barrel. At
least we have our shootin' irons strapped back on."

"Yeah, well, we're outnumbered, less'n you count Jake
Ward."

"I don't know if we can count on Jake Ward just yet. He's
green as a willow branch."

"He wants Hobart bad as we do, Johnny."

"Maybe. But I don't know what he's made of yet. I don't know if his backbone has iron in it or just tallow."

"How are you going to find out?" Ben asked, genuinely puzzled.

"The only way you can see a bear's teeth is to make him mad as hell."

"You aim to make Jake mad?"

"I'm going to tell him just how Hobart gunned down Jesse. He'll see it like we saw it and he'll smell the blood and hear his brother scream. By the time we get to Tucson, I'll know if we can count on Jake's help."

"If we get that far with this bunch," Ben said.

"We'll get that far," John said.

Ben shook his head. "Feels like we'll be riding straight to hell with these owlhoots. One sniff of who we really are and what we aim to do and they'll gun us down without batting a damned eye."

"So play along, Ben. And stay away from Jake."

"Why?"

"If anything gives us away, it'll be him. Like I said. He's green as a young crab apple."

"You got me worried now, John."

"Good. Stay that way."

"You ain't worried?"

"For the first time in weeks, I feel real good, Ben. These boys are going to lead us straight to Hobart."

"And then what?"

"And then, I'm going to send Ollie Hobart straight to hell."

7

JUBAL MEAD PULLED OUT THE MAKINGS FROM HIS POCKET, GRAB-bing the loop of the string with one tooth as he fished out the papers. He unfolded the packet, wet the tip of his finger, and stuck it to the top layer of thin paper. In his left hand, he formed a trough of the paper. He put the paper packet back in his pocket, stuck his index finger in the sack opening until it widened. He shook tobacco into the paper and leveled it with his thumb. Then he pulled the loose string taut until the sack closed. He put the sack back into his shirt pocket. Then he rolled the paper back and forth until he had the right consistency, folded the short end inward, rolled it up to the other end, held the ends tightly, and licked the seam with his tongue. When he was finished, he stuck the quirly into his mouth.

"You got a lucifer, Cruddy?"

"I gave you a box of matches yesterday, Jubal."

"Yeah. Left 'em in my other shirt."

Crudder handed him a small box of matches.

The men smoked, their faces barely lit by the fire inside the hogan. Mead struck a match, lit his cigarette, and handed the box back to Crudder. He looked up at the diamond-strewn sky. It seemed close in the clear air, the Milky Way a vast carpet of silver clusters that blinked like signal mirrors.

"What do you think of those new men, Jubal?" Crudder asked.

"Not much."

"You think we could use 'em?"

"For what?"

"Ollie wants a bunch of men, he told me. Got something big planned."

"Ollie scares hell out of me," Mead said.

"You don't trust him?"

"About as far as I could throw a damned anvil."

"He's fair with his men, I hear."

"Yeah, then how come he don't have none?"

"The ones he had with him made some mistakes, got themselves killed."

"That bothers me some," Mead said.

"Luck of the draw," Crudder said. His face was covered with lumps as if he had been bee-stung. The lumps moved when he talked, giving some the impression that there were worms or some other flesh-eating bugs under those doughy bulges.

"Your tally goes a long way with me," Mead said, his florid face wreathed with blue smoke from his cigarette. He had a barrel chest and a thick neck that had a goiter bulge in it from drinking too much beer and eating too much fat. He was never far away from an open bottle of one kind or another.

"Ollie is a gold hound," Crudder said.

"Huh?" asked Ward.

"He can smell gold."

"Oh, I get it," Mead said. "Like a bloodhound. Only he smells gold."

"That's what I mean," Crudder said, sparks from his cigarette wafting off the tip like golden fireflies.

"Gold has no smell," Horky said.

"For Ollie it does," Crudder said. "He don't dig it or pan it, though. He finds them what does and then takes it. You heard what he done up in Coloraddy?"

"I heard," Mead said. "Got him quite a poke."

Ward stiffened at the mention of the massacre that involved the death of his brother. These men did not know he had any connection to that slaughter and robbery. But he was interested in what Crudder had to say about Hobart. He had never met Ollie, but he wanted the man to pay for what he had done to all those people, including his brother, Jesse.

John and Ben came outside, their shadows stretching long ahead of them. The outlaws stopped talking and watched as they came up, joining them under the canopy of stars.

Ben pulled out his pipe, filled the bowl with tobacco, and tamped it tight. Crudder struck a match and held it out to him.

Ben put the pipe in his mouth and leaned forward. Crudder touched the flame to the pipe tobacco. Ben's cheeks caved in as he drew on the stem.

"Thanks," he said.

"You don't smoke, John?" Crudder said.

"Never picked up the habit."

The other men laughed.

"You don't know what you're missing," Mead said.

"Yeah," Ward said, "a sore throat, a morning cough, a bad taste in your mouth."

All of the man laughed.

"It all goes away with a swaller of whiskey," Mead said, and the men laughed again.

"We got us a kind of storehouse over yonder," Crudder said, pointing to one of the adobe dwellings. "You get yourself some candles and pick out an adobe to sleep in tonight.

"They can bunk with me," Ward said. "I've got candles, plenty of room to lay out their bedrolls."

"All right," Crudder said. "If they can stomach your snoring, Jake."

More laughter from the group.

"I don't snore," Jake said. "Those are rats you heard."

"Rats don't sleep at night," Mead said. "They're too busy gnawing at my nuts."

The men laughed some more.

John thought they were pretty much at ease in the dark canyon with its brooding walls and total isolation. They didn't act like outlaws, but maybe that was because none of them possessed a conscience. Like Hobart's men. He couldn't understand how such men could live happy lives, always on the run, always looking over their shoulders. No jobs, no homes. Maybe the life appealed to certain kinds of men, but not to him. He wanted to get rid of Hobart and hang his gunbelt on a wooden peg and grab a pair of plow handles, turn the earth, and plant seeds. Maybe find a nice girl, marry her, and raise cattle and corn and such. He wasn't much better off than these owlhoots right now, he thought. He was on the run, too, homeless, rootless, chasing a murdering man who had caused him so much grief.

At the moment, he thought, he was no better than any of the men around him. He just had a different purpose in life, that was all. But maybe he wasn't any better than they. He wanted to kill a man, rob him of his life. The line between him and the outlaws wasn't so thick after all. In fact, it was as thin as a reed.

"Well, I'm going to turn in," Crudder said, dropping the last of his cigarette to the ground. He pressed it flat with the heel of his boot and started walking toward one of the dark adobes.

"Good night, Cruddy," Mead said.

"Yeah, good night," the others chorused.

"Come on, John and Ben," Ward said. "We'll get your bedrolls and get us some shut-eye."

The group broke up. Horky and Mead slept in the hogan where the cook fire basked, keeping the fire alive during the night. John and Ben carried their bedrolls to Ward's adobe. He lit candles and they found places to sleep.

Jake lit three candles, handed one each to Ben and John.

"We won't talk tonight," Jake said. "Our voices carry too much in this canyon. See you in the morning."

"Good night, Jake," John said.

"Good night," Ben said.

"I wouldn't try to run off if I were you," Ward said. "For

all his joviality tonight, Crudder would kill you as soon as look at you."

"We're not going anywhere," John said.

"You wouldn't get far."

"I know."

"And one more piece of advice, John. Don't take your boots off tonight. I killed a bark scorpion yesterday morning in here. Shake out your bedroll in the morning and check it tomorrow night if we're still here. The little buggers like to hide in blankets, boots, and dark places."

"Thanks, Jake," John said. "I never saw a scorpion before. Did you, Ben?"

"Yeah, back in Missouri. Little bitty things. They got a stinger on their tails."

"They're as deadly as a rattlesnake," Ward said. "So watch your step."

Ben and John scoured the place where they lay their bedrolls before laying them out on the ground.

Ward lay down, placing his pistol close at hand. He blew out his candle and laid it on the ground within easy reach. He turned over and closed his eyes.

Ben and John lay down, their heads close together. John held a finger to his lips and mouthed the word "wait."

Ben nodded.

John blew out his candle. Ben snuffed his out with his finger, waxing the tip and part of the nail. The oily smoke hung in the air for several moments. John heard Horky and Jubal talking, but couldn't make out what they were saying. Soon, they stopped and it grew quiet.

John lay there, his eyes open, fighting off sleep. He listened to Jake's breathing and to Ben's. He reached over and jostled Ben to make sure he was still awake.

Jake's breathing became deeper, more even. In a few minutes, he began to snore.

John waited another five minutes, then felt for Ben's head. When he touched his ear, he scooted closer, whispered into it.

"You awake, Ben?"

"Yeah."

"I don't trust this bunch."

"Me, neither."

"We've got to get away from Crudder whenever he takes us out of here."

"He can lead us to Ollie Hobart."

"I know. But Crudder is a dangerous man. And sooner or later, he'll find out who we are."

"What do you want to do?"

"Just follow my lead. I'll get shut of him before we get to Tucson. We can track him to Hobart."

"Hobart will know we're comin', John. Crudder will sure as hell put a bug in his ear."

"Can't be helped."

Jake's snoring became louder.

"Just let me know when you plan to make the break."

"I will. Might have to run for our lives."

"Won't be the first time, Johnny."

"No. And it probably won't be the last. Now, get some shut-eye."

"You, too," Ben said.

John lay awake for another half hour. Finally, the snoring subsided to a tolerable drone in his ears and he sank into sleep. His right hand gripped his pistol. It was a comfort, something he could rely on. But maybe Horky had been right, closer to the truth than any of them knew.

Perhaps, he thought, as he drifted into sleep, the gun was cursed.

It was sure that it had blood on it.

8

CRUDDER MADE IT EASY FOR BEN AND JOHN.

The following morning after breakfast, when the men were all drinking a second mug of coffee, Crudder announced his plans.

"We can't all ride into Tucson in a bunch," he said. "We'll draw too much attention to ourselves."

"So what do we do?" Mead asked.

"We got a meetin' place. We drift in at night, two at a time. Meet up at the Lobo Rojo, that little cantina on Vera Cruz."

"I don't know where it is," Ward said.

John blew steam from his tin cup and sipped his coffee, his gaze fixed on Crudder. He and Ben didn't know where the cantina was, either.

"You find Hidalgo Street, ride west. You'll come to Vera Cruz. Head north three blocks. You'll see the Hotel Norte. Right next to it is the Lobo Rojo, a big sign on the false front and a big red wolf on it."

"When?" Mead asked.

"We should get to Tucson tonight," Crudder said. "I'll go in first, take John Logan with me."

John felt a squeezing of his heart, as if Crudder had reached into his chest with a grimy hand. He drew in a breath to ease the pressure.

"Horky, you and Jubal ride in about an hour later, from the south trail. Jake, you'll take Ben with you and come in from the northeast where that old trading post stands."

"I know the place," Ward said.

"An hour apart. We'll all ride together until we're five miles out, then split up. I should hit town a little after sundown."

"Will Ollie be expecting us?" Mead asked.

"He goes to the Lobo Rojo ever' night," Crudder said. "Toward midnight. Far as I know, he's stayin' at the Norte."

"I hope this works," Mead said.

"It'll work. Just watch out for yourselves comin' in to town. Don't draw attention to yourselves and don't throw down on them Injun police."

The men laughed and finished drinking their coffees, each locked in a silence with his own personal thoughts. John cursed the fact that he would have to ride in with Crudder. But it might work out. They should be at the Lobo Rojo long before Ollie Hobart showed up. The bad part was that he and Ben would be separated until they all met up at the cantina. There would be no chance to hatch a plan.

Ollie would recognize him on sight, John knew.

The men packed up and stored the things they would not need on their ride to Tucson. Horky took Ben and John to get their horses in the natural corral through the fissure in the canyon wall. Crudder, Mead, and Ward saddled their horses. Well before noon, with Crudder in the lead, the men were all riding single file back out of the hideout. It was cool until they reached open country, and then the sun beat down with a merciless heat until men and animals were glistening with sweat.

Crudder behaved like a military man, and John learned that he had fought in the war on the Union side. He had been at the battle of Elkhorn Tavern, which some called Pea Ridge, and at Wilson Creek, up near Springfield, Missouri.

He sent out flankers, Mead and Ward, and put Horky on point. Ben rode drag. John rode with Crudder for the first couple of hours, then gradually slowed down so that he could talk to Ben.

There were no road signs, not even much of a road, and the country was unknown to Ben and John. Crudder did not stop but had told the men to chew on jerky in the saddle. He pressed on, seemingly unmindful of the heat that boiled up from the shadeless earth.

"You got any plans, John?" Ben whispered to John when they were riding side by side.

"I can't go to that cantina with Crudder, I know that."

"Well, you could. But you'd have to be mighty quick the minute Hobart walks in the door. You'd have to take both him and Crudder down."

"Hobart will be on home ground."

"Yeah. Maybe Crudder, too."

They could taste the faint dust stirred up from the hooves of Crudder's horse. The air itself smelled old, John thought, musty as the atmosphere in an old abandoned house. Yet the harsh land seemed to glow with a hidden radiance that was complemented by the blue sky and the floating puffs of white clouds. It was a majestic land, he decided, made even more interesting by the sudden outcroppings of buttes and spires and deserted mesas, the exotic plants that seemed to rise out of the ground at odd places and grip the land firmly as if defying a waterless existence.

"We've got to get away from this bunch before we hit Tucson," John said. "There's no other way around it."

"Horses can't run much in this heat, John."

"I know. We'll have to find a way to elude Crudder, make it too costly for him to chase after us."

"You have some kind of a plan, Johnny? Or is that askin' too much?"

"You can keep the sarcasm, Ben. The country here, just look at it. Wild, broken, plenty of hiding places."

"Empty as last year's bird nest."

"We'll use it, nevertheless."

Ben twisted his head to one side, then the other, to take in the width and breadth of the land. He could see the flankers, and in the far distance, he could just barely make out the point rider. And Crudder, maybe two hundred yards ahead of them. Whoever had staked out the road had picked the path of least resistance. Yes, there was broken land, pocked with rocky rises and formations, but none were real close. They'd have to ride miles to find suitable cover, a defensible position. Surely, John could see that. It might be like this all the way to Tucson. He shook his head and wiped sweat from his brows. Any of the men ahead of them could pick them off with a rifle shot before they galloped a hundred yards.

If they made a break for it now, Ben thought, they'd be dead meat.

"I just don't see no way," Ben said.

"Not now. We'll have to let the land tell us when it's time to make a run for it."

"The land ain't tellin' me nothin' but heat and sweat."

"The Indians made use of it, Ben. And so will we."

"They was born here." Ben could not put a hobble on his sarcasm. John let it pass because he knew Ben was right.

"Sometimes, Ben," he said, "if opportunity doesn't come knocking, you have to kick the door down yourself."

"I never heard that before."

"Me, neither. I just thought of it."

Ben snorted.

John continued to survey the land, an empty feeling in the pit of his stomach.

Giant saguaros stood like green sentinels, silent and strangely sentient, as if they could see and feel in their muteness, their deafness, and their blindness. They seemed alive and somehow comforting as they stood amid the seeming desolation of that barren landscape. Off in the distance, John could see shadowy monuments rising up from the plain, their rock walls like fortresses, their secrets lost to time and an emptiness he could feel deep inside him. He drew a deep breath and knew he could never explain the feelings he had just then. They were too complicated, too hazy and unformed, like snatches of a dream he could reach for but never touch.

Ahead, Crudder rode on and John could see that his head was drooping, as if he were half asleep, dozing in the saddle.

The bastard, John thought, he feels safe with the two out-riders and a man on point, Ben and John covering his rear. Complacent, perhaps.

He could feel the land rising under him, so gradual it was barely discernible, but he sensed a subtle shift in the air, somehow a half a degree cooler than it had been. He wondered if they were climbing toward higher ground, ascending from the desert ever so slowly.

A trick of the mind? He didn't know, but he looked at the western horizon and it seemed higher than it had before, as if they were riding toward a small summit. He looked behind him and it seemed to him that he was looking down, down into that long gradual valley they had just traversed. They were climbing. He was sure of it. The walls of the canyon where they had been were now only dim and small battle-ments reduced to rubble and ruin as if they were sinking out of existence.

There had to be a way to escape Crudder and his men. It was too bad they couldn't talk to Ward and bring him along. Another gun to go up against Hobart and the bloodthirsty men he gathered around him. How many men, he did not know. But Hobart was, for all his faults, a leader, a man who surrounded himself with heartless and greedy cohorts who would do his bidding.

"You're awful quiet, John," Ben said after they had ridden for another half hour. "Workin' on a plan?"

"Maybe," John said.

"If we come close to one of them high-walled mesas, we might have a chance to make a run for it."

"They'd shoot us right out of the saddle. Too open, Ben."

"Then, where? Hell, the old sun's already fallin' away from high noon."

John gave Ben's question some moments of thought be-fore he answered.

"We're riding an outlaw trail, Ben. Way off the old Butterfield Stage Trail to Benson. There has to be some reason owlhoots picked this route. There are mountains yonder, and we're close to the Mexican border. Somewhere, between here and Tucson, we'll find a way to light a shuck away from these jaspers. Let the sun fall. The closer we get to dark, the closer we get to a place that will suit us just fine."

"Boy, Johnny, you sure give a man confidence. Ever had any luck a-wishin', bettin' on horse races?"

"I believe this, Ben. You make your own luck. Good or bad."

And that was where they left it as they both looked for opportunity's bold knock on their door.

When it came, John Savage would jerk the door right off its rusty hinges.

9

THE LAND AROUND THEM CHANGED AS THE LONG VALLEY DISAP-
peared behind them. Ahead and all around lay hills and
small mountains, broken country. The kind of country, John
thought, where a man might make a break for it and disap-
pear behind any number of hills. To the south lay Mexico,
and perhaps safety. A good day's ride, maybe thirty miles or
so, two days at the most.

He looked at Ben, whose eyes were as wide as an owl's.

"You thinkin' what I'm thinkin'?" Ben asked.

There was a hollow feeling in the pit of John's stomach.
He knew that he was on the verge of having to make a life-
or-death decision. If he made the wrong choice, he and Ben
could be killed. They were outnumbered and they had to tra-
verse a considerable distance to outrun both bullets and men
on horseback. But the prospect of being with Crudder when
he met up with Hobart was almost as distasteful as risking
his life.

"We can't run the horses much, Ben," John said. "This heat
has sucked out all their energy."

"I know," Ben said. "But if we're going to break away
from this bunch, this looks like pretty good country for it."

"Ever been to Mexico?" John asked.

"Nope."

"We might have to hole up over the border for a while."

"Makes no nevermind to me."

John scanned the country to the south. More and more hills rose up and there were jagged peaks beyond, low mountains that looked forbidding. And, maybe, sheltering.

"When we get close to a bunch of those hills, we'll light a shuck," John said. "You stay right on my heels. I'm going to zigzag in case we have to dodge bullets."

"I can zig and I can zag," Ben said, the crinkle of a smile on his lips.

"Don't follow my exact route, Ben. When I zig, you zag."

And John was smiling when he said it. But Ben knew he was dead serious.

"I'll do that, Johnny. You just say the word."

A half hour later, John said the word.

"Now," he said and wheeled Gent into a tight turn, not forty yards from a peaked hill. Ben clapped his spurs to Blaster's flanks and the two men rode toward the east end of the hill, gobbling up ground in a furious gallop.

They heard a shout from Crudder. When John looked over his shoulder, he saw the man stop his horse, back it down. He pointed in their direction, then jerked his rifle from its scabbard.

"Get 'em," Crudder yelled, and his voice carried across the plain, rippling with his anger and determination.

Ten yards from the corner of the hill, John heard the whip-crack of a rifle. The bullet spanged off a rock a few yards behind him and caromed off into the air with a nasty whine. John pulled hard on the left rein and Gent swerved a few yards before John reined him back to a straight line. He drew his pistol, turned slightly in the shadow, aimed high at Crudder, and fired off a shot. He knew the bullet had little chance of hitting its target, but it might give the man a reason to hold off his pursuit for a few moments. And it might slow down his reloading of another cartridge into the firing chamber.

John rammed his pistol back in its holster and rounded the end of the hill. There were many more hills ahead of him and all around him. He rode into the maze, Ben hot on his heels.

Just as Ben reached the end of the hill, another shot rang out and John heard the bullet slam into the hill. He looked back and saw that Ben was still coming. He was bent over the saddle horn and seemed untouched and unhurt.

John raced toward another hill and turned Gent so they could round it. He slowed the horse after passing the hill and Ben caught up to him.

Both men were panting, out of breath. The horses' sides were heaving.

"Enough of that fast gallop," John said. "From now on, we pick our way south real slow."

"Think Crudder will come after us?"

"He might for a ways, but he'll give it up. If we go real slow, we won't leave much sign on this hard ground. Unless he's a damned good tracker, he'll give up."

They rode through a series of narrow passes, through small and slightly larger hills, varying their direction, putting more hills behind them. John watched their backtrail and drew his rifle. If he saw Crudder or any of the others come around a hill, he would stop and draw a bead, try to drop the pursuer.

"Crudder fire that last shot at you, Ben?"

"I—I think so. Couldn't tell. What are you thinkin'?"

"Jake was on the flank. I hope he didn't shoot at you."

"Aw, he wouldn't do that. He's on our side."

"He might have loosed a bullet to throw Crudder off. Jake won't want to show his hand."

"Hell, he should be ridin' with us."

"No. Better that he stay with Crudder and that bunch. If we get to Hobart, he might come in handy."

"Yeah. He might."

They heard pounding hoofbeats, shouts. It was difficult for John to determine how close Crudder and his men were because of the hills. He and Ben walked the horses south for several moments, cut in and out of saguaros and hills, their horses sleek with sweat, their foreheads dripping wet. They sopped up the moisture with their bandannas and rode on, keeping quiet, listening, looking over their shoulders.

"These horses need rest, John," Ben said, his voice a croak in his parched throat.

"I know. I don't see any shade, do you?"

"Can't we just stop and give 'em a rest?"

"Might be our last stop, Ben. No telling where Crudder is. He might know this country. Hell, he could be waiting just up ahead for us."

Ben swore.

"Hey, don't talk that way, Johnny. My stomach's still tied up in a hundred different knots."

"Just keep quiet and keep riding, Ben. We'll stop when we've lost Crudder for sure."

John headed toward a low hill, crossing a patch of rocky land dotted with prickly pear, saguaros, ocotillo. Something caught his eye and he turned suddenly in the saddle to seek out the source. A glint of light, like a spear, needled him in his right eye. He raised a hand to shade his face. He looked upward, toward a peak jutting up, its top framed by blue sky.

"Ben," John said, his voice pitched low, "watch it."

Ben turned and looked at that same peak and swallowed hard.

"We been snookered," Ben said, shading his eyes with a hand.

One of the riders, John didn't know which at that distance, was at the top of the peak, looking down on them. Sunlight glinted off the barrel of his rifle as he brought it to his shoulder and took aim. The horse under him sidled on unsure footing and the rifle came down for a moment, then rose again to the man's shoulder. John saw him sighting along the barrel.

In the fraction of seconds it took for the man to steady his horse and take aim, John judged the distance between him and the muzzle of that rifle.

At least two hundred yards, maybe more, he figured.

A hundred thoughts flashed through John's brain in those

meager seconds. Distance. Trajectory. Angle. Windage. All useless, all numberless. But he thought of them and wondered if the man on the hill was a marksman. If it wasn't Crudder, he would have sent his best shot up there, a man who could drop game at four hundred yards or maybe five hundred yards. Who could shoot a running rabbit, bark a squirrel, take a turkey's head off with a .30-30 at one hundred and fifty yards.

That was likely who was up there on that peak, and he and Ben were out in the open, no cover that would stand up to a lead bullet that could go through a saguaro and tear a man's heart to shreds.

"Zigzag," John barked and wheeled Gent just as he saw a puff of white smoke belch from the muzzle of that rifle.

Ben rode off in one direction. John rode off in another.

He heard the crack of the rifle after the bullet struck near the spot where he had just been a split second before. He didn't look back and rode for the little hill, twisting Gent back and forth like a corkscrew. A few seconds later, he heard the whine of a second bullet as it caromed off a rock, and the rifle report sounded like an afterthought in the stillness.

He reached the hill and reined Gent behind it as another shot sounded. He did not hear the bullet and hoped it had not hit Ben.

Ben rounded the other end of the hill and John pointed straight south. The horses were struggling to keep up speed, and he knew they could only go a few more yards before one or both of them foundered.

It was a dangerous time.

More figuring in his head. How long would it take the shooter to ride down that hill and give chase? How stout was the man's horse, how much wind did it have left?

Questions and more questions, hurtling at lightning speed through his mind as if any of the answers could save them.

And where were the other three men?

"We got to hold up, John," Ben said. "Or we'll kill these horses."

"Do it," John said, hauling on the reins. Gent stumbled to

a halt and hung his head, gasping for breath, the air wheezing in his throat, his sides heaving with the effort to draw cool air into his lungs. Only the air was not cool, but hot and thick, burning already tortured tissue.

"He'll be comin' after us, John."

"Probably. Let's walk them south and we'll make a stand behind the next hill.

Both men looked ahead as their horses plodded along, out of breath, out of strength, and out of fight for survival. It pained John to hear Gent struggling for breath and feel him walking on wobbly wooden legs that were about to turn to rubber.

There was nothing but empty plain ahead.

The landscape was as desolate as if a giant thrasher had swept it clean of all life. The hills were on either side and far away. South were gullies and washouts and stately saguaros standing mute as statuary.

John jerked his rifle from its scabbard, then hauled on the reins, pulling Gent to a full stop.

"What're you gonna do, Johnny?" Ben asked.

"I'm going to shoot the first sonofabitch that rides around that hill."

Ben stopped, turned Blaster around, and pulled his rifle from its scabbard.

Neither man said a word as they waited. Waited for whatever was bound to come.

10

FAR OFF IN THE DISTANCE, TO THE SOUTH, JOHN SAW SOMETHING that startled him. It was so far away he could not be sure what it was. The only thing about it that caught his eye was the color. Green. He felt as if he was looking at a far-off sea, the way the light bounced off the verdant patch of land. He closed and opened his eyes as if to clear his brain of mirages, false images.

When he opened them again, the color was still there, and his heart throbbed in his temples for a moment. So small, so far away, but the contrast of that color against the bronze brown of the surrounding landscape made his heart skip a beat as if some drug had invaded his veins and pumped some exotic fuel into his bloodstream.

"Somebody's comin', Johnny," Ben said, his voice a whispery rasp.

John looked back toward the hill they had rounded. A man on horseback was heading their way, his rifle barrel glinting in the sun.

"Yeah," John said.

"It looks like that Mead feller."

"It is."

"Where you boys goin'?" Mead called. "Don't y'all want to come to Tucson with us? Make you some money?"

Ben and John exchanged glances.

"No, Jubal," John yelled back, "we have other plans."

"You got Cruddy mighty upset, runnin' off like that."

"Let Cruddy ride his own trail," John replied.

"He don't like folks he treated real nice runnin' out on him."

All the time he was yelling, Mead was walking his horse closer to them. John noticed that, measured the distance, gauging the range.

"We don't like to be told where to go," John said as Mead closed the distance a foot or two at a time.

"He thought you'd be grateful."

"Grateful for what?"

"Well, he didn't kill you boys."

"You're right about that, Jubal," John said. "All he did was kidnap us and keep us prisoner."

Mead guffawed. Coming closer.

"He's inchin' up on us, John," Ben said.

"More like yarding up on us, Ben."

Ben didn't laugh.

"Why don't you and Ben ride on back with me and talk to Cruddy? See if we can't settle this." Mead kept coming.

"Nothing to settle," John said. He no longer had to shout.

Another few feet and he'd be able to see Mead's eyes. They were shaded now by the brim of his hat.

"Yeah, I think there is," Mead said, his horse eating up more ground.

"We can't just let him . . ." Ben's voice trailed off.

Jubal Mead stopped his horse. He was raising his rifle to his shoulder.

John's hand dove for his pistol. Mead was well within pistol range. John's hand was a blur as he cleared leather, cocking the pistol on the rise.

Ben swore under his breath.

Mead steadied his rifle. John could see him clearly.

Mead fired his rifle.

Ben ducked instinctively.

John raised his arm, took deadly aim with his pistol. As Mead was levering another cartridge into the chamber of his Winchester, John squeezed the trigger. The pistol bucked in his hand with the recoil. Smoke and sparks belched from the muzzle and the bullet sped on its way. Mead looked up as the bullet caught him square in the chest.

Mead's arms rose up and the rifle in his hands took to the air. He looked, for an instant, like some lost supplicant beseeching the heavens for mercy. It was a terrible moment for John as he let out the breath in his lungs.

He cocked his pistol for another shot, but Mead was finished. He clutched at his chest and swayed to one side, then toppled to the ground. His rifle fell nearby with a dull thud.

"You got him, John. Put his lamp out, sure as hell."

John said nothing. He looked at the fallen man. Mead was not moving. His horse had backed away and, head drooping, ears stiffened, looked at the dead man, whickering softly. The sound of the horse tore at John's heart. There was a sadness in that whicker, a note of animal grief over a lost friend.

John put the pistol on half cock, rammed the empty hull out of the cylinder chamber, and shoved another cartridge into the empty spot. He spun the cylinder and seated it. He kept six bullets in his pistol, unlike some, who left an empty chamber on which the hammer could rest. For safety's sake. He left the pistol on half cock and slipped it back in his holster, a sudden sickness in him that had no known origin nor residence.

He looked at the dead man as if to raise him back to life, but Mead lay there, his body stiffening in the sun.

"He ain't goin' to get up, John," Ben said, as if reading his thoughts. "We ought to light a shuck. Them others'll be swarmin' out here like a pack of hornets."

"Yeah," John said, just to be using his voice instead of thinking about Mead and the bullet that had taken his life.

Did talking about a thing make it so?

John wondered.

Perhaps, he thought, there was a curse on the gun his father had customized for him. Maybe there was a curse born of that day when Hobart and his men had gunned down his entire family—father, mother, little sister—and he had taken up the gun to exact vengeance.

Have I kept the pistol with honor? He wondered. *Have I only drawn it with good reason?*

Maybe.

"John, we ought to git," Ben said. "You can't do nothin' for Mead."

"I know."

Ben tickled Blaster's flanks and turned him to the south.

"Well, come on, then," Ben said.

John clucked to Gent and turned him, following Ben, the sickness gradually subsiding. That is, the queasiness in his belly was diminishing, but there was a cloud of it in his brain, a worry that flitted around inside the cloud like a wounded bird, a broken-winged fledgling sparrow that had fallen from its nest and could not fly. The gun weighed heavy on his gunbelt and he could feel its pressure against his leg, the heat from it burning through to the bone.

"See that green spot yonder?" John said to Ben when they had ridden some distance from where they had been.

Ben squinted into the sun, shaded his eyes.

"Might be one of them mirages."

"Do you see it, damn it?"

"Ain't no need to get testy about it, John. Yeah, I see somethin' green way off. Don't look real, though."

"Well, head straight for it. Might be grass, and where there's grass, there's probably water. And where there's water, there are probably trees."

"Whooo-ee, John, I think that sun done burned your brain to a crisp."

"Just hold to that line, Ben."

"You are testy, ain't you?"

John said nothing and when Ben looked over at him, Ben turned away as if unable to bear the look on John's face.

They rode on in silence, both looking back every so often

to see if they were being followed. They were not, but the uneasiness between the two men continued. For no good reason, Ben would have said, but he was keeping his mouth shut.

The green patch grew as they rode closer. It spread from a small island into a peninsula, but they still could not make out what it was. The ground was uneven. It rose and fell like some undulating reptile, and they did see small shimmering lakes dancing in the sun, looking like lakes or ponds. The heat was intense and both men were oiled in sweat, their foreheads grimy and glistening, their shirts black with moisture and stuck to their backs and drooping sodden in front.

The valley was lower than the terrain the two men were traversing, and when they came to its rim, their eyes widened in wonder. Spread out before them was a long valley, lush and green with grass and a sea of wooly sheep clustered at one end. There were adobe huts, like small islands, on the far side and in the middle and near them. They saw no signs of life, neither herders nor sheepdogs, and they rode down into the grass and saw the irrigation canals threading through the grass, little silver threads among the green.

"A sheep ranch," Ben said.

"Looks like it."

John scanned the horizon. The sheep were feeding. He had no idea how many there were, but they covered a large section of land and seemed so peaceful and contented, he wondered if his eyes were playing tricks on him.

"There's a little canal near that adobe over yonder," John said. "Let's give the horses a drink and see if anyone's home."

"It don't look natural, does it?" Ben said, tipping his hat back and scratching behind his ear.

"It's mighty strange. But somebody went to a lot of trouble to bring water and grass to the desert."

"I'll say," Ben said.

They rode down to the nearest adobe shack. It looked old,

as if it had been there for centuries. The bricks were smooth and crumbling, but the roof had not been thatched that long. It was small and had but one window on their side. As they rode around it to the front, there was a side window, too. But the adobe looked deserted.

In front, there was a bare patch of ground where no grass grew, and a pot of flowers next to the door. The ground looked trampled, as if it had known many feet of late.

"Hello the house," John called as the two men reined up. The horses nickered and shook their heads, their rubbery nostrils sniffing the nearby water. Gent looked longingly at the ditch where fresh water ran from east to west. Both ends curled back into the grass in the shape of a horseshoe.

"Anybody home?" Ben called, a note of uneasiness in it.

"Door's closed," John said, "but it doesn't look tight."

"Nope. It's open a crack."

"Well, let's go see. Maybe somebody's asleep inside." John swung out of the saddle and led Gent to the ditch. The horse drank greedily, the bit clicking against its teeth.

Ben dismounted and took Blaster to another spot and let the animal drink.

John walked up to the door and pushed on it. It swung on leather hinges, but it was too dark to see inside.

He started to step through the door, when he heard a slight sound.

The next moment, he was staring at the twin snouts of a double-barreled shotgun.

He heard two clicks as someone on the other end hammered back.

Ben froze to a statue.

John's muscles tightened and then loosened as instinctively his right hand dropped to the butt of his pistol. This happened so fast, he wasn't even aware of what he had done, but his mind was clanging with warning klaxons and he knew he was just a split second away from getting blown to shreds at close range.

"You jerk that pistol, mister, and you'll be nothin' but blood and bone lying in a pile of rags."

John's fingers went numb as his gut roiled with a sickening bile and his knees turned to jelly.

He looked into the darkness and saw only a black chasm where a man might tumble into eternity in the solitary blink of an eye.

11

BEADS OF SWEAT GLITTERED LIKE AMBER ON JOHN'S FOREHEAD, glistened like a cluster of tiny jewels. His pulse pounded in his ears. His heart raced with a runner's speed. Beyond the barrels of the shotgun was a darkness as black and cold as a mine pit, and the abyss beckoned to him with all the hypnotic power of a hooded cobra weaving a dancer's arabesques as it rose slowly from a fakir's woven basket.

Time stood as still as the caught air in his lungs.

He raised his right hand with a slowness beyond measure. He opened his palm to show that it was empty. Sweat seeped into his eyes, stinging the delicate tissue with the acrid breath of shaven onions.

"There you go," the husky voice said. "That's a nice boy."

John tried to swallow the hard lump in his throat.

"Now, step back, sonny. Real slow-like."

John took a step backward. The ground felt like a sponge under his boots, as fragile and shaky as a suspension bridge over a deep canyon.

Next, John heard a shrill, high-pitched whistle from inside the adobe.

"Both of you, keep your hands high, where I can see 'em."

Ben's hands shot upward and John let his float to a place above his head. Men rose up from places in the surrounding grass. They all held rifles and they advanced slowly toward the two men. They were Mexicans and their bronzed faces bore menacing looks. They seemed to appear from out of nowhere. He heard the soft squeak of leather as the door to the adobe opened wider.

"Now, let's see you boys try something," the voice said.

John saw something move and then a person stepped out, holding the shotgun.

The person was a woman. She was wearing duck pants and boots, a bright blue gingham shirt, and a straw hat. Her hair was snowy white, dripped down her back in a single braid. She wore a pistol and gunbelt. John stared at her in disbelief.

"Now, what have we got here," she said. "A couple of sheep rustlers?"

Ben swallowed and said nothing.

"No, ma'am," John said. "We're not rustlers, honest."

The Mexicans, six of them, surrounded John and Ben, their rifles held at the ready, hip high.

"Then, what the hell're you two doin' on my property? Sneakin' around, tryin' to break into my line shack?"

"Ma'am, if you'll ease those hammers down on that scattergun, I'll tell you why we came onto your property."

"Mister, I don't trust you as far as I could throw your horse. You just tell me what you're doin' here and you'll keep breathin'."

"Some outlaws are chasing us, ma'am. We were just riding south to get away from them."

"That what the shootin' was all about? I heard some shots a while ago."

"Yes'm," John said.

"You kill anybody?"

"Yes'm."

A look of suspicion crept into the woman's eyes.

"Who'd you kill?"

"One of the outlaws. He was drawing down on me with his rifle."

"And you shot him?"

"Yes'm, I did."

"So you say."

"So I say."

"You look like an owlhooter yourself. You and that old codger there."

"I know," John said, and his lips formed a wry smile. "But do we look like sheep rustlers?"

The woman cocked her head and eyed John with one raised eyebrow.

"Hell, I don't know," she said. "You look like my kid brother. And he's a no-account scoundrel."

"Yes'm," John said.

"What's your name?" she asked, and from her tone, John thought she really cared.

He wondered if he should lie and tell her the same story he told Crudder. He didn't like to lie, especially to a woman. Especially to a woman with a shotgun in her hands.

"I'm John Savage. My friend's name is Ben Russell. We're chasing a man who killed my family and others, stole all our gold out in Colorado."

The woman pursed her lips and wrinkled her nose. Shadows crept into her eyes, vanished. She blinked as if to regard him with a fresh look.

"You're that John Savage? We heard about you down here. You've killed a lot of men."

"Yes'm. Have you heard the name Oliver Hobart?"

"Who hasn't?" she said.

"Well, he's in Tucson. The men who were chasing us are joining up with Hobart. Led by a man named Crudder. Ever heard of him?"

"No, can't say as I have. But Hobart is a wanted man—a killer and a thief."

John said nothing, waiting for the woman to digest all the information he had given her. It did not take long.

She eased the hammers down on the shotgun and stepped toward John.

"I'm Gale Gill," she said. "I'm a widow, and this here's my ranch. I raise sheep on land my husband bought from the Navajo. Come with me. I'll take you to the house and we can drink some *tepache*, cool down some. Would you like that, John Savage?"

"Yes'm, we'd both like that."

She spoke to the Mexicans in Spanish. All but two walked away.

"Juan will go with us," she said. "You and Ben can walk with me. He'll take your horses to the corral, give 'em water and corn."

"That's mighty nice of you, ma'am," John said.

"Call me Gale. The name's like the wind, sonny. Spelled that way and meanin' that way."

Gale lived in an octagon house that lay nearly a mile distant. There were corrals, a small barn, a wagon, horses, and a fence to keep the sheep out. A stream ran past the house and down to the river.

"Yonder's the border," she said. "As hostile as any place on this good earth. Come on in."

John and Ben followed Gale into the house, struck by its simplicity and its sturdiness.

"Your husband build this?" John asked.

"We both did, and it cost us a pretty penny for the lumber."

John sat in a comfortable homemade chair that was cushioned and covered with deer hide. Ben sat on the small sofa that was similarly made, while Gale sat in a large rocker that seemed to diminish her already small size. She took off her hat and laid it on the small table at her side. A young girl drifted silently into the room. John saw that her feet were bare. She was Mexican, or Indian, he thought, from her high cheekbones and dark russet skin.

"Chula, bring us three cups of *tepache*, will you please? And tell Juan to come in when he's finished putting up the horses."

The girl nodded without speaking and left as silently as

she had come. John could not even hear her feet touch the polished hardwood floors.

There was a large bookcase that covered one wall, with leather-bound volumes neatly arranged. In one corner stood a small rolltop desk that was open. There were papers stacked on it and an inkwell with a pen sticking out at an angle. The room smelled of wisteria and lilacs and something indefinable, perhaps leather or wood.

"I want you to listen to Juan Torres," she said. "He can tell you a thing or two about Oliver Hobart. And maybe you can tell him a thing or two."

"Yes'm," John said, removing his hat. He darted a glance at Ben, who took off his hat and set it in his lap. John put his on the floor. He saw the rifle over the fireplace, just above the mantel, and a box of cartridges beneath it. A Colt pistol in a holster, with a filled gunbelt, dangled from a wooden peg at the end of the mantel. All within easy reach, since the fireplace was small and a woman the size of Gale could easily stand on the hearth and grab the rifle. He was pretty sure it was loaded. It was polished until the bluing gleamed, and it was unmistakably a Winchester '73.

Chula brought the drinks out on a round wooden tray, handed one to Gale, and one each to Ben and John.

"Thank you," John said.

"Juan is coming," she said to Gale in perfect, although accented, English.

"Send him right in, Chula."

"Do I give him the *tepache*?"

"No, he is working."

Chula did not bow nor reply. She just left the room on those silent feet of hers. She was like a cat, John thought. She moved with grace and was probably older than she looked. She seemed self-assured. He wondered what she was doing in the house. He heard no sounds from the other rooms. Perhaps she did not cook, he thought. Perhaps she sewed, mended clothing, or wove shirts from wool gathered from the sheep.

She was very pretty and looked no more than eighteen, but might have been twenty or so.

She reminded him of his little sister and he felt a sudden pang in his heart, thinking of little Alice, cold in the ground, so needlessly slaughtered by that bastard Hobart.

"Tastes good," Ben said after a swallow of the sweet *tepache.* "Nice and cool."

"We make it in a clay jar, what the Mexicans call an olla. Mix beer and fruit and let it ferment under a damp cloth. The olla keeps it cool. Won't get you real drunk, but it'll make you right happy."

"It is good," John said. "What are all those books up there?"

"My husband, Clarence, liked to read and so do I. Some of the books, a very few, are mine."

"Yours?"

"I wrote them," she said. "And if you look through those magazines on the shelf, you'll see my name. Just got one from *Harper's Weekly* the other day. I write stories and novels."

"That's amazing," Ben said.

"What? That a woman can write books, too? Just like a man?"

"No, ma'am," Ben said. "I just meant I never met no real writer before. I seen a reporter or two, but no real book writer."

Gale laughed.

"I don't knit or sew, Ben, so I write books instead. Keeps my mind occupied when I'm not running off rustlers or no-accounts."

John heard a door open and close at the back of the house. Then, footsteps sounding on the floor and down the hall. A moment later, Juan Torres entered the room, his hat in hand.

"Sit down, Juan," she said.

She patted a spot on the divan next to her and Juan sat down.

Juan sat very straight. He had a patrician nose, high cheekbones, soft dark eyes, and thin lips cutting across tight skin as if his head had been sculpted out of copper. He had small

hands, but they were calloused from hard work. He wore a
white shirt and pants, like the other Mexicans, muslin, John
thought, but perhaps cotton woven very thin.

"Juan, that man there is Ben Russell and the young one is
John Savage."

"Savage?" Juan said. "From Colorado?"

"Yes. He's hunting Oliver Hobart."

Juan's already taut face tautened even more. A light
danced in his eyes like some lambent sparkle from a dark star
far out in space. His lips tightened and thinned. His hands
clenched into fists.

"You are hunting Oliver Hobart, Mr. Savage?" Juan said,
his accent faint as a wave sound in a seashell. The accent
was there but hard to trace.

"I am," John said. "I mean to kill him when I find him."

"You cannot do this, Mr. Savage. You cannot kill Hobart."

"Why not?" John said.

Juan took a deep breath and a sadness came into his eyes
like a cloud shadow passing beneath the sun.

"Because . . . because . . ."

And he could not go on. He bent over and began sobbing
softly. Gale put an arm over his shoulder and drew a deep
breath as if fighting off tears of her own.

Juan pulled himself up and stopped crying. He wiped a
sleeve across his eyes and smeared moisture from his cheeks
with a swipe of his hand.

The room filled with a silence that was so thick, John felt
he could touch it. And if he did, it would be like touching
stone.

Cold, hard stone.

12

JUAN TORRES SHOOK HIS HEAD AS IF TO THROW OFF THE LAST OF his tears. He blinked his eyes dry and looked at Gale.

"Go ahead, Juan. Tell Mr. Savage why you don't want him to kill Oliver Hobart."

"I tell you," Juan said, "if you go after Hobart and try to kill him, he will kill my sister."

"Your sister?" John stared hard into Juan's eyes.

"He stole her, and when I try to get her back, he tell me he will kill her if anyone try to take her away from him."

Ben and John exchanged knowing glances.

"You can see, can't you, John, that this is a most delicate situation?" Gale said.

"Yes."

"So you must not jeopardize that young woman's life. It would devastate Juan and his family. And I would never get over it, either."

"Neither would I," John said.

"It is good that you understand," Juan said.

John looked at Juan, his lower lip edging up over the upper. His eyes narrowed to dark slits as he pondered the situation. He knew how Juan felt. He would feel the same way.

He had seen what Ollie Hobart had done to his mother and sister. He knew that the man was cruel and heartless, even with women.

"Juan, I will promise you this. Ben and I must have a showdown with Hobart. But we won't go barging in with our guns blazing and throwing lead. As long as your sister is in danger from him, we won't make a move. But we must get this man. We must stop him or he will go on killing and robbing people. Do you understand me?"

"Yes, but I am still afraid."

Gale patted Juan's knee in reassurance.

"Juan and I both understand perfectly. Nobody is safe around here as long as Hobart is allowed to live and go on killing and stealing. But you both must surely know what you are going up against when you go after Hobart. Two of you cannot possibly stop such a man. He has a gang of gunslingers around him and outnumbers you, three or four to one."

"We know that," John said. "When Ollie attacked our mining camp, he had several men with him. Ben and I went after him. Just the two of us. We managed to get most of them."

"Yes, but not Ollie himself," Gale said.

"No."

"And some of his men chased you here, so you said."

"Yes. They're going to join up with Hobart. That's true."

"We got one of 'em," Ben said.

"And one of those left may be on our side," John said.

"What do you mean?" Gale asked. "Might be on your side?"

John told her about Jake Ward.

"So he wants to kill Hobart, too," John said, finishing up his account.

"Might be he'll save you the trouble," she said.

"Could be. I don't care who gets Hobart. I just want him to pay for what he did to all those people, including my folks. Pay with his life."

"An eye for an eye," Gale mused.

"Yes, something like that."

"Well, we can talk about this in the morning," she said. "I want to make sure you weren't followed here, and Juan has to get back to work tending the sheep. There's a bunkhouse out back. You want to stay over, I hope."

"Yes'm, we could use some rest and time to think. I may have a way to draw Hobart out in the open, away from Juan's little sister."

"I'd be right interested in what you have to say. Want to take supper with me tonight?"

Ben and John both nodded. Gale smiled.

"Fine. We'll eat about six of the clock."

"Yes'm," John said.

The bunkhouse was small, made of adobe. It had cots and blankets in it, nothing else. There were six army cots inside it and two of those were taken.

"Looky here, will you, John?" Ben said.

There, in a corner, were their saddles, bedrolls, rifles, and saddlebags. Their bridles hung on wooden pegs driven into the soft brick.

"Seems like Mrs. Gill knew we'd stay with her," John said.

"I reckon so. Better check your saddlebags, John. Them Mexes find our gold and . . ."

"You check them, Ben. I trust these men who work for Mrs. Gill."

"You do? After all we been through, I wouldn't think you'd trust nobody."

"It's Gale Gill I trust. A woman running a sheep ranch this size has to be pretty strong. I figure her men have taken on some of her character.

John lay on one of the cots and stretched out his legs. Ben rummaged through all four saddlebags, sounding like a huge pack rat going through a wooden box.

"Ain't nobody touched nothin'," Ben said. "Our gold and our money is right where we left it."

John smiled, but said nothing.

When Hobart had robbed the mining camp, he missed a

cache hidden in John's father's tent. John had kept the sacks of dust and the nuggets, cashing in small amounts only when he and Ben needed money to continue their pursuit of Hobart. John was glad that they still had quite a bit of gold. Maybe now was the time to put it to good use.

It was cool inside the adobe. Bare as it was, it was the most comfortable place they had seen in a long while.

"Johnny, you got any idea how long we'll be stayin' here?" Ben was lying on a cot, his blanket under his head for a pillow.

"Long enough for me to work some things out."

"What things?"

"Juan and Gale were right. We can't just go galloping into that cantina after Hobart. Juan's sister could be killed in the cross fire. Or Ollie would put her lamp out just for pure meanness."

"Hell, that warn't my idea in the first place. I thought we'd just wait outside somewheres until we spotted the bastard and then let him have it."

"You can bet Ollie's thought of that. He knows we're after him. He'll know it for sure once Crudder blabs to him."

"Crudder don't know who we are. He thinks we're the Logans, dumber'n a pair of stumps."

"Ollie will figure it out. He's smart."

"Maybe."

"No maybe about it, Ben. No, we have to think this through."

"You're the one with the thinkin' cap, Johnny. I can't hardly figger out how to get through the day."

John laughed. "You do all right," he said.

"Well, you got any ideas buzzin' around in that head of yours?"

"A couple."

"I'd like to hear 'em."

John sighed.

"Still working on them, Ben. Maybe by supper. You know, this ranch was a surprise to me. Green grass and all. Sheep. I'll bet this country holds a lot of secrets. It's an old land. Indian land. Like that canyon we were in with Crudder. The Navajos, Hopis, or whoever they were, lasted a long time with Kit Carson chasing them all over. I want to ask Gale about this ranch and the country."

"What good will that do?"

"I don't know. We might find out a few things."

"You got somethin' in your craw, Johnny. I can tell. You hold your damned cards pretty close to your vest, son."

"Sometimes that's the best way. I don't have any cards yet, though. I'm just shuffling the deck at this point."

"Well, I'm goin' to get some shut-eye. Wake me if you have somethin' important to talk about."

"I will, Ben, I surely will."

Ben slept until supper time when John awoke him. They washed up at the pump in back of the house, heard the sheep bells tinkling in the distance, the bark of a dog. The sun had smeared the western sky with splashes of gold and crimson, dusted the clouds with silver and purple, bronze and vermillion. It was quiet and there was a breeze blowing cool across the burning land.

"You set a fine table, Gale," John said when they sat down to supper. The smell of mutton and gravy assailed his nostrils, stirred his salivary glands. Ben was grinning at the lavish spread, his eyes bright as sun-shot agates.

The girl who had served the *tepache* brought more food and drink, hot coffee and cakes for dessert. Gale treated Chula like a daughter and she also sat at the table, only getting up when something was needed from the kitchen.

"I have some fine brandy from Santa Fe," Gale said when they had all finished eating. "We can sit in the front room where it's cool. Open those front windows, will you?"

Chula nodded.

When they sat down, Chula served brandy in delicate snifters.

"You're spoiling us, Gale," John said, holding the glass to his nose, sniffing the vapors that arose from the dark liquor.

She swirled the brandy around in her glass, holding it with the reverence of a chemist, raised the glass up to her face, and closed her eyes as she drew in the aroma. She looked as if she might be holding a bouquet of flowers, sniffing the scents. Her hand was beautiful, John thought, strong and delicate as any he had ever seen.

Chula lit a lamp as the evening shadows began to flow into the room like a soft fog, even though it was still light out.

"The brandy reminds me of home and that takes away some of the loneliness," she said.

"Yes'm," John said. "Where are you from originally?"

"Texas, where the tall pines grow."

"Never been there."

"I miss seeing the hickory nuts fall in the spring, the smell of pine trees. Ever since Clarence was taken from me, I miss the little hills, the green trees, the change of seasons."

Ben looked as if he might cry.

She took a sip of her brandy and leaned back, looked at John.

"We built this place so that the front faces east, just like the Navajos. We got that much from them and a lot more, I suppose. I miss seeing the sunsets, though, at this time of day, in this room. But in the morning, the sun streams through the windows and you feel happy to be alive."

John said nothing. His mind was working in a divided state. Her words made him homesick for Missouri, even the high country of Colorado, but he also wanted to talk to her about the plan that was forming in his mind.

"I'm lucky to have what I have," she said. "And mighty grateful, too. But I do get lonely of an evenin', sure as the grass grows tall on the prairie. I miss old Clarence, the folks back home. But I love the sheep and the men who work for me, men who have never seen a Texas sky or a catfish pond."

She sniffled and took another sip of brandy. She looked out at the soft evening forming as the shadows darkened and seeped into the room, bending away from the oil lamp.

"John," she said, "how do you plan to take down Hobart, knowing what you now know?"

She switched the topic so suddenly, John was caught by surprise.

He had a plan in mind now and the brandy had worked in him so that it blossomed in his mind like a garden of spring flowers.

"I might need your help," he said. "I do have a plan to draw Hobart out in the open. You won't be at any risk, and I think Juan's sister will be safe."

"I hope that head of yours is more than just something to hang a hat on," she said. "But, sure, if I can help, I'm ready, willing, and able. Just what did you have in mind?"

"Gold," John said. "Hobart lusts after gold and I think I know a way to make him come to me, just like he did back in Colorado."

Gale looked at him as if he'd lost his mind. So did Ben.

"Gold," John said again, "and salt. That's what I aim to do."

"Salt?" Ben said.

"Did you say salt?" Gale asked.

John smiled at both of them.

The flame in the lamp flickered with a sudden waft of breeze through the windows and the shadows outside darkened into night and settled a deep hush over the land in that strange alchemy of transformation when known things changed into unknown shapes and all landmarks disappeared.

It was a perfect time to speak of his bold plan, a time when dreams could take on form and substance and seem attainable.

"I'm going to need an old mine," John said, "somewhere close to Tucson. An abandoned mine, if you know of one. Any old abandoned mine will do."

Ben and Gale both drew in breaths and stared at John with pitying looks usually reserved for the very feeble-minded, or the insane.

13

TO A RAPT AUDIENCE OF TWO, BEN AND GALE, JOHN SAVAGE LAID out the rudiments of his plan.

"If we can find an old abandoned mine shaft," he said, "somewhere in the mountains around Tucson, I can set it up real quick. We salt the mine, haul some rock into the assay office in Tucson. The rock will have enough gold in it to start the gossip. Gold, to humans, is nectar to bees."

"Where you goin' to get all this gold?" Gale asked.

"Won't take much. And we have some we can lay our hands on. Ollie will get the word."

"That ain't goin' to work, John," Ben said.

"Why not?"

"Ollie ain't a hard-rock miner. He steals the gold."

"I know. That's where Gale can help us, if she will."

"You'll have to explain," she said.

"We'll need a little shack put up near the mine, with a clear field of fire. We'll let the assay office know that we're using cyanide. We'll buy some in town, other equipment, and tell them we're handling the ore ourselves, turning it into gold, keeping it to ourselves."

"Hmm," Gale said. "It's getting more interesting. Go on."

"We'll have a smokestack, burn oil and wood in it during the day, so people can see it. We'll get the word out that we've struck a huge vein, the mother lode, maybe. Ollie won't be able to resist. He'll come after that gold he thinks is there."

"It'll take some time to set up, do all that you want to do," she said.

"A month or so, maybe."

"Hell, John, Ollie will see you go in to town, know it was you at the assayer's. He'll smell the fish."

"It won't be me," John said.

"Then, who?"

"I'm hoping Gale will be the one to take the raw ore in that we salted. She's known hereabouts. People probably trust her. They'll think she's been prospecting all these years and fall for it."

Ben let out a low whistle.

"Might work at that."

"If I agree to do that for you," Gale said.

"I'm hoping you will."

"How soon," she said.

"As soon as we find that old mine and buy it or stake claim to it."

"There are a few old mines around Tucson, up in the hills, the mountains. Silver, mostly, that petered out. But some that were blasted for gold. They could be bought cheap or claimed, as you say. I'll give it some thought."

"Would you?" John said.

"Consider it done. I'll do some checking in town. About time I rode in and got some supplies anyway."

"Ben and I will have to lay low until we find such a mine," John said.

"You can stay here long as you like."

"I'll pay your men for the work they do."

"Oh, we can get men to do the job if you pay them. Won't take much probably."

"I'll pay them well," John said.

The three of them talked long into the night, going over every inch of John's plan.

"I like your idea, John. It so happens that my husband was once a hard-rock miner. What's more, we still own the mine. He took silver out of it and was sure there was gold somewhere in the mountain. But before he could blast deeper into his tunnel, the cave collapsed and killed two men. He couldn't go on, and he never got over it."

"Close to Tucson?"

"Very close," she said.

"We can make it work, maybe."

"What's more, John," and there was a flicker of a smile on her lips, "we had a laboratory on the property. Everything is still there, just as it was. A little cleaning, some dusting, and you'll have a lab that will smelt silver, separate gold from ore. There should still be cyanide in there."

"Your husband must have found some gold, then," John said.

"He did. Just beyond a vein of silver, he knocked out a chunk of rock that was laced with gold. He thought there might be a mother lode somewhere under that mountain."

Ben slapped his knee.

"By golly, it just might work, Johnny. You got a mine, a lab, and we got the gold to salt it with."

"What happened to that chunk of rock your husband dug out?" John asked. "He ever get it assayed?"

"No. He didn't have the heart. I still have it, in fact. It's in my bedroom. Kind of a nest egg for a rainy day, I guess."

"That's a start," John said, "if you'll let me use it. That'll get the ball rolling."

"It's yours," she said. "I really hope this works. I want to see Hobart pay for what he did to your family and get that girl back unharmed."

"Can you take us to the old mine tomorrow?" John asked.

"Bright and early."

John and Gale shook hands and said good night. Ben talked all the way to the bunkhouse, as excited as a kid with a new toy. John kept silent, going over his plans in his mind, anxious to set a trap for Hobart, bring him to his gun sights, and end, finally, the long bloody hunt. By the time Ben and

John got to the bunkhouse, it was after midnight and the coyotes were singing, the sheepdogs barking.

John slept fitfully that night, awakening several times in the middle of disturbing dreams, dreams that made sense while he was dreaming, but flew away in confusion when he opened his eyes to the darkness. He dreamed of defective pistols that would not load, would not shoot. He dreamed of young mahogany women in dim-lit saloons, with shadowy figures looming over them. He dreamed of dogs chasing him across a desolate landscape and stars raining silver and gold into a burning lake where he was flailing in the flames, unable to swim, his throat parched so raw he was unable to scream.

One of the Mexican sheepherders in the bunkhouse shook him awake very early.

"Es la madrugada," the man said.

It was dawn, but the sun was not yet up and, outside, the sky was a pale ember in the east, golden and pink along the horizon. Far off, he heard the bleating of sheep as he wiped grit from his eyes and shivered against the chill. He woke up Ben and they both smelled coffee on the currents that threaded the still air, errant tendrils of tiny zephyrs that blew off the mountains and died in the caverns of their nostrils.

Lamps glowed inside Gale's home, orange and yellow light pouring feebly through the windows, signs of life in a land of shadows. Ben sniffed as they walked to the pump next to a watering trough behind the house.

"Smells like breakfast," he said. "My belly has done heard the call."

"Your belly always hears the call," John said.

In the distance, some few hundred yards from the house, they saw an open fire, and behind it, a chuck wagon. The sheep bells tinkled beyond their vision and the land seemed to slowly slide into motion as herders tramped toward the chuck wagon to the tune of yapping dogs.

A door opened in the house. Gale stuck her head out.

"Grub's on the table," she said and disappeared.

Moments later, Ben and John were sitting at the breakfast

table, buttering biscuits, slabbing on honey, drinking coffee, and cutting up boiled mutton and green beans.

"That red stuff in the jar there is hot sauce," Gale said. "What the Mexicans call *salsa casera* or *salsa picante*. We grow our own food here, including the chili peppers."

"I'll have some of that," Ben said and poured the sauce on his mutton.

Moments later, his eyes watered and went wide from the sting of the sauce on his tongue, the burn in his throat.

John and Gale laughed.

"It'll sure clean out your system," Gale remarked.

Gale's horse was a stocky steeldust gray she called Moonbeam, and she led the way on an old trail that circled the grazing sheep.

"All this was Navajo country," she said, "until Kit Carson drove 'em all to reservations. Some said he wished, later, that he hadn't done it, but if he hadn't done it, none of this country would have ever been settled. They were a murderin' bunch."

"Any problems now?" John asked.

"No, the tribes are pretty well cut down and scattered. Biggest fear in them days was their habit of stealin' sheep. My husband and I came here, prospectin', but we found this place and started in raisin' sheep. It's been good to me, and to him while he was alive."

"You must miss him," John said.

"I do. But I keep him close by. In my heart."

They rode through the long shadows of morning, into rugged, mountainous country, filled with the green sentinels of saguaro, iron-laden rocks, and various kinds of cactus plants. Jackrabbits jumped and bounced on each side of them and quail piped from ocotillo outposts.

A little past noon, they rounded a small mountain nudged by several smaller hills and a mesa that jutted out like the prow of a ship.

Gale pointed to an object atop the mesa.

"There's the laboratory," she said. "Just beyond that, in the face of the mountain, is the mine. Good road up there, if it hasn't been washed out."

"Where's Tucson?" John asked.

"Ten miles north of here. See that wagon road yonder?"

John and Ben looked. The road was still partially in shadow, but plainly visible. It stretched across a wide plain bordered by hills and jumbles of mountains and rocky spires. John felt his breath catch in his chest.

"Pretty close," Ben said.

"It's tempting," John said, "to just keep riding and put the barrel of my pistol right in the center of Hobart's forehead."

"And pull the trigger," Ben said.

"You're both savages," Gale said without mirth.

"Naw, John's the savage," Ben said. "I'm a Russell."

They started up the wagon path to the mesa, butting between that outcropping and a small rocky hill.

John wondered at the truth of Ben's words. He did want to kill Hobart. The thought was like an iron fist in his brain. His hatred for the man threatened to consume him, blot out all else. Yet he knew he must wait, must bide his time. He had changed, he knew. Before his parents and sister had been murdered, before the slaughter at the mine, he had never thought about killing a man.

Now he thought of little else.

And that thought bothered him. Had he turned savage? Heartless?

Maybe the name Savage fit more than he would like it to.

Maybe, he thought, his name was his destiny.

And the hunt for Hobart, his fate.

14

THE LABORATORY GLISTENED IN THE SUN WITH ITS BLEACHED dry lumber grayed by wind and rain and scorching sun, a clapboard relic from another time. Its old frame seemed solid enough when John rode around it, tapping on the odd sized boards with his fist. The boards were all cut to different widths, from four inches to a dozen or so, and the tin roof was rusted to a nut-brown hue, held to the frame with sturdy bolts.

"He built it fine," John said as he dismounted. "You got a key for that lock on the door?"

"Yes," Gale said, climbing down from Moonbeam. She wore a leather bag slung over her shoulder and took out a large key. The lock was rusted, too, but the tumblers clicked into place and she was able to pull it open. She and John walked inside while Ben held the horses.

Gale stepped inside, held the door wide for John. Light spears lanced through the large room from the grimy windows, cracks that had opened between the wall boards, from nail holes that had widened in the roof. The floor was packed earth. There were tables all about, sturdy work tables, and scales, cruets, bottles, cans. A large stove stood at the back wall, its chimney going straight out instead of straight up. The chimney was reinforced with tin and there was tin on the back wall behind the stove.

"That's a little smelter, I guess," Gale said. There were rockers and sledges, hammers, chisels, a host of tools that could be used to break rock or pry raw gold loose from ore.

John saw at least three anvils, ore buckets, some full of rock, others turned over on their sides, empty. There was a wheelbarrow, shovels, picks, a stack of firewood, at least four cords, stacked inches from one wall, candles, miners' hats with candles, boxes of candles, matches, oil lamps, oil. There were boxes of dynamite and boxes of caps, fuses, gloves lying on tables and shelves, some short-handled mauls, a small cookstove, pots and pans, and plates complete with knives, forks, and spoons.

"Looks like he had everything he needed," John said, watching the golden dust motes dance in the spears of light.

"Clarence was very thorough. There's more stuff up in the mine. Probably just as he left it. Want to walk up?"

"Yes. Should I bring a lantern or take a tin hat?"

"Might be a good idea. I don't know how far back the mine goes."

"I'll take a couple of lanterns," he said.

Gale and John went back outside, carrying lanterns filled with coal oil and matches to light them.

"Found a place for the horses," Ben said. "Over yonder's a hitchrail." He pointed to some posts and rails near the cave entrance.

"Meet you there," John said.

Ben rode Blaster to the railing, leading Moonbeam and Gent by their reins. Small puffy clouds floated beyond the mountain in a dazzling blue sky. Quail piped from the next hill and a hawk floated on an air current down to a small rocky canyon. The quiet was broken only by the crunch of John's boots on gravel and the soft pad of Gale's small boots on a sandy path.

"How long has it been since you've been up here?" John asked her.

"I came up here about a year ago, just to check on things. I don't know why. Who would bother with an old abandoned mine?"

"I guess mining's pretty well over with in this country."

"No, there are a few mines here and there. Just not anywhere near here. I don't know. Clarence may have been wrong about that mother lode. And he never did have that chunk of ore assayed. And I lost heart after he died."

"How did he die?"

"Oddly enough, he was killed by a Navajo, some throwback who came through with a small band and tried to steal our sheep. He came up to the house, him and six or seven others, and offered to buy some sheep. But he had no money. He said his name was Mano Rojo, Red Hand, and he said he'd pay Clarence in a moon or two."

"He wanted credit."

She laughed.

"He didn't use that word. He said we were on sacred ground and owed him the sheep. When Clarence asked him how he was going to pay for the sheep, Mano said he would kill a white man and rob him."

"Pretty bold of him," John said.

"Clarence told him to go away. He would not sell him any sheep on those terms. Mano left, but he took thirty head of sheep with him. Clarence gave chase and Mano shot him dead. The Mexicans who were with Clarence said that Mano boasted to them that he had paid for the sheep just as he said he would."

"Did anyone ever catch Mano?" John asked.

She shook her head.

"No. He got clean away, the bastard."

"Ever see him again?"

"No. The authorities in Tucson put native trackers out, but they came back empty-handed. Mano and the sheep disappeared into thin air, I guess."

"I'm sorry."

"He'll turn up someday. The Navajos claimed a lot of territory in their day. They're nomads. He'll be back one day and I'll be ready for him. He's got blood on his hands and he'll pay for what he did to my Clarence."

"Kind of the way I feel about Hobart," John said.

They spoke no more until they reached the mine adit. By then, Ben had tied up the three horses and was standing just outside the entrance, looking at something just inside the cave wall.

"Ben, here's a lantern. Light it up."

John handed one of the lanterns to Ben, but he didn't even look at it. Instead, he pointed to something on the wall.

"Looky here, John. Somebody's done drawn some pictures on this here wall."

John and Gale stepped up and peered at the spot where Ben was pointing.

Gale's face blanched when she saw the drawings. She looked as if she was going to faint, and he put an arm around her waist to hold her up.

"Mighty curious," Ben said, still staring at the etchings.

John looked up. There were crude drawings there, cut into the rock with a knife or a flint blade. They looked to be fairly new, with none of the weathering one would expect from an ancient site.

"Those are Navajo petroglyphs," Gale said, almost gasping. "Rock carvings done by them savages."

"What does it mean?" Ben asked, turning around.

"You can figure it out if you look real hard," Gale said. Color came back into her face.

"Were these here from olden times?" John asked.

She shook her head.

"No, these are less than a year old. See the sheep? See that hand dripping? See the rifle and the bullets shooting from the barrel? And that's Clarence, I'm sure, that stick figure falling off his horse."

"Well, I'll be damned," Ben said. "Who's Clarence?"

"Her husband," John said. "This was cut into the rock by a Navajo, maybe a brave named Mano Rojo, Red Hand. He stole her sheep and shot her husband."

"Damn," Ben said.

"He's been here," Gale said. "And he put that there to brag. He knew I'd probably see it someday. It might have been here a year ago, but I doubt it. Those cuts look pretty fresh."

"Did he know this was your husband's mine?" John asked.

"I don't know," she said. "Maybe." She looked around at the hills, the lab, the horses standing hipshot at the hitchrail. "He could be watching us this very minute."

Ben looked around, too.

"I don't see nobody," he said.

"Let's light these lanterns and have a look inside the mine," John said. "Gale, you can stay here if you like, keep an eye on things. I'll get your rifle."

"No, I'm going in with you. Maybe Mano stayed here. If so, there'll be sign."

John set his lantern down on the ground and knelt to light the wick. Ben did the same, while Gale walked to her horse and pulled her rifle from its scabbard. She returned as the lanterns began to glow.

"Let's take a look," she said.

"Maybe we better get our rifles, too, John," Ben said.

John looked at Gale. She nodded. "Might be a good idea," she said.

"All right, Ben. Bring them. Just to be on the safe side."

Ben pulled their rifles from their sheaths and the three walked into the mine. John and Ben held their lanterns high to throw light ahead of them. The shoring began about thirty feet inside, and the mine narrowed. There was only room for one person at a time, and John took the lead, handing his rifle to Gale.

"I can draw faster than I can set the lantern down and cock that Winchester," he said.

"You think somebody's in here, John?" Ben asked, a slight quaver in his voice.

"No, Ben, I don't. But I'm just as spooked as you are. Reminds me of the mine we had over in Colorado."

"This one's been worked a lot more," Ben said.

Gale brought up the rear, John's rifle over one shoulder, hers at her side.

"It splits off into two shafts," she said, "just ahead."

"Then what?" John asked.

"Take the one that goes to the left. That's the one where Clarence found the gold."

The end of the shaft appeared some thirty yards past the fork. The corridor was wider there, and had been shored up with heavy timbers. John held the lantern with both hands and moved it over the rock face. At one point, he held the lantern in one spot and moved in closer to see. There were little gold flecks surrounding a place where a chunk of rock had been removed. The flecks flickered like frozen fireflies in the stone.

"Is that what I think it is?" Ben said.

"Hard to tell," John said. "It sure looks like gold."

"I'm sure it is," Gale said, standing on tiptoe to look.

Ben moved his lantern in closer and the three of them examined the area surrounding the hole. Some of the specks in the rock reflected silver, or mica, perhaps quartz, and the flickers were like small stars embedded in rock.

"There could be a vein or two beyond this point," John said. "What do you think, Ben?"

"It sure looks right promising," Ben said. "Some hard picking might show more color than we see now."

"You've seen something like this before?" Gale asked.

Both men nodded.

John lowered the lantern and stepped back.

"Let's see what's up that other shaft.

The three retraced their path to the fork in the shaft. John entered it with Ben close behind. He had not gone very far when he stopped short, staring at the floor of the shaft. This one was wider than the other and Ben stood beside John. He slowly raised his lantern.

There, on the ground, were blankets and wooden canteens, boxes of rifle and pistol cartridges, stones set in a small ring that were charred and smoked.

"Let's get the hell out of here," John said.

"What's the matter?" Gale asked, a note of alarm in her voice.

"I can smell their sweat," John said. "Somebody's living in this mine."

Gale craned her neck to see and then drew back in shock.

"Those are Navajo blankets," she said.

"Quick," John said. "They could be back at any time."

Gale turned around and started back toward the entrance.

"Be hell to get trapped in here," Ben said, following close behind her.

They reached the entrance. Sunlight blinded them for a few seconds as they stepped outside. John looked toward the hitchrail. The horses were still there.

"Oh no," Gale cried. "Look."

A lone rider appeared on the mesa, just beyond the lab. He rode a pinto and his head was wrapped with a yellow-and-red bandanna. He carried a rifle and was wearing a breechclout over his duck pants. He wore moccasins and, dripping from one side, a pistol and holster secured around his waist by a gunbelt.

The Navajo saw them, raised his rifle above his head, then turned his horse and disappeared over the ledge.

In the distance, there was the squealing *scree* of a hawk and then an immense silence, except for the trip-hammer throb of heartbeats in three pairs of ears.

15

SOME YARDS AWAY FROM THE CAVE ENTRANCE, JOHN SAW A PILE of rocks stretching some seventy or eighty feet. It appeared that whoever had worked on the mine had carried the rocks in a wheelbarrow, starting at the farthest point on the ledge and dumping them in a straight line. The rock piles were waist-high and would provide them some cover.

"Ben, give me your lantern and get behind those tailings over yonder."

Ben handed John the lantern. John set both lanterns on the ground, grabbed his rifle from Gale. "Go over there where Ben is," he said. "Get down behind the rocks and keep your rifle pointed toward the edge of the mesa where that Navajo popped up."

Gale ran to where Ben was waiting and lowered herself to a kneeling position. She balanced the barrel of her rifle on a rock, aiming it toward a point where the road ended atop the mesa.

John ran to the horses and removed all three sets of saddlebags. He slung two of them over his shoulders and lugged the other in his left hand. He grabbed the canteens, then started toward the broken rocks.

He saw a slight movement out of the corner of his left eye. A split second later, he heard the crack of a rifle. Flame and smoke belched from the snout of a gun and a bullet whined over his head, smacked into the mountain. There was a clatter of rocks where the ball had hit as they tumbled down. John dove for the shelter of the tailings as another shot rang out. The bullet plowed a furrow in the ground just behind his path and spurts of dust kicked up in a thin spout that quickly evaporated.

John lay there, panting, his heart pumping in a rapid, steady beat.

"Almost got you that time, Johnny," Ben said.

"You see the shooter?" John gasped, gulping in air.

"He ducked back behind that lab building. Never got a good look at him."

"It was an Indian," Gale said.

"How many you figure, Gale?" John asked.

"I don't know," she said. "At least two, probably more. I'm glad you brought the saddlebags. We could be stuck here for a good long while." She had packed their lunches that morning and stored them in the saddlebags.

They waited, the hot sun beating down on them. John listened intently for any sound from the lab or below the mesa. He heard only the distant call of a quail and the rustle of the breeze over the rocks, a soft whisper that only emphasized the deep silence. The horses shifted their weight on their rear legs, switched their tails at flies, and let their heads droop in the heat.

Then John saw movement. It was so slight he almost missed it. He stared at a clump of brush, sage, he thought. It didn't move. He blinked his eyes to bring the plant back into focus. He stared at it until his eyes burned. He closed them, then opened them again. Had the bush moved? He could not tell. He looked to the right and to the left of it as if to fix it in that spot. There was a large rock on one side, a prickly pear on the other. He now looked at all three as he listened to the sound of his own breathing.

Moments passed by and the silence stretched into an eerie

stillness that seemed somehow unnatural. Ben cleared his throat. John shot him a look and held a finger to his lips. Ben wore a sheepish look, but nodded. Gale scanned the ground around the laboratory and the entire rim on three sides.

The more John looked at the clump of sagebrush, the more suspicious he became. It was a large clump, and seemed to be composed of two different kinds of plants. He couldn't be sure, but as he looked around the plain, he saw that all of the plants were small, much smaller than the bush that had attracted his attention.

He scanned the ground behind the plant but could not tell if the ground was level or humped. He thought there might be someone lying behind the plant, someone who had moved it slightly a while ago, moved it enough so that he had been able to detect that ever-so-slight motion. Was it just a gust of breeze that had made the plant quiver? That could be, he thought. But if that was what had happened, why had his gaze been drawn to just that particular clump of sage? If a wind had coursed across the ground, wouldn't all of the living plants have been touched by the fingers of that zephyr?

He moved his rifle, set the front sight on the bush, lined the blade up with the rear sight. He held the rifle right against his shoulder and blocked out all but that one bush. He closed his left eye. He fingered the trigger, then realized that he had not levered a cartridge into the chamber. Should he?

As he stared down the barrel and over the gun sight, the bush moved.

Ever so slightly. An inch, two inches. No more.

John held his breath, stared hard to make sure.

He opened his left eye and gauged the distance between the rock and the prickly pear in relation to the clump of sage.

The bush had moved. Definitely.

John cleared his head, his thoughts racing through options and possibilities with the speed of a bee heading for the hive.

He levered a cartridge into the firing chamber of his Winchester. He left the hammer back at full cock and kept his gaze on the brush clump.

"What is it, John?" Gale asked in a whisper. "You see somethin'?"

"I don't know," he said.

"Ain't nothin' out there I can see," Ben said.

"That's just it," John said. "There's nothing you can see, but there's something out there. A Navajo, I think."

"Where?" Gale asked. John could tell that she was startled by the apprehensive tone of her voice.

"See the big clump of brush, looks like sage and maybe mesquite or a tumbleweed? Biggest plant out there."

"I see it," Ben said.

"I see it now," Gale said.

"It moved," John said. Then, after a pause, he said, "I think."

Gale and Ben stared at the sagebrush for several seconds.

John wiped a sweaty palm on his denims, then scrubbed the stock with his sleeve to dry it. Sweat shone on his forehead and he wiped it away with his left hand.

"I don't see nothin'," Ben said. "Johnny, you're spooked. It's just an old clump of sagebrush, that's all."

"No, it isn't," Gale said.

"Huh?" from Ben.

"John's right. There's sage there and some other kind of bush, like it was put together to bulk it up. Else it growed that way."

"See anything behind it?" John asked. "Like a man lying on his belly?"

Both Ben and Gale were silent for several seconds.

"Nope," Ben said. "Looks just like brush to me. Can't see nobody behind it."

"Hard to tell," Gale said.

John looked again, but could not discern anything resembling a man lying behind the bush.

He kept looking, but he was thinking, too.

"You know how hard it is to see a jackrabbit when it's just frozen? I mean you can look right at it and not see it."

"Yeah. They're hard to see," Ben said. "Cottontails, too, if they freeze up."

"Any animal," Gale said. "You can look straight at a deer in the woods and never see it, lessen it flicks its tail or twitches its ear."

"Well," John said, "if there's a Navajo flattened out behind that bush and he doesn't so much as twitch, he's going to be mighty hard to see."

Neither Gale nor Ben said anything, but they were nodding their heads.

"I think there's somebody there," John said softly. "I can feel it."

"Sometimes your gut tells you," Ben said, a nervous quaver in his voice. He, too, spoke very softly.

"I've got an idea," John said. "It might not work."

"Tell us, John," Gale said. "I'm plumb out and I still don't see nobody out there."

"This goes beyond whatever I think is moving that brush toward us," John said. "I'm going to shoot it, but then I want you both to cover me while I make a dash for that laboratory."

"You're crazy, John," Ben said. "If there's somebody out there, you'll be a big target."

"I think there's only one and I think the rest are waiting to see how he does. Maybe he wants to steal our horses and then they'll just starve us out."

"What makes you think that?" Gale asked.

"Sometimes you have to think like your enemy," he said.

"Why are you going to the lab?" she asked.

"That's closer to the rim of this shelf, and there are things in there I can use."

"Like what?" Ben asked.

"Dynamite for one," John said. "We can't just sit here and bake in the sun, wait for them to rush us. There may be only two or three Navajos down there, or there may be two dozen. From what I know of them, they're not afraid to die. That makes them mighty dangerous."

"You're right there," Gale said.

"So if I shoot and jump a Navajo brave, I'll keep shooting until he drops. Then I'm going to run as fast as I can to that lab and go inside. You two will have to fire your rifles pretty steady until I make it."

"How will we know you've made it?" Gale asked.

"I'll send some smoke up that chimney," he said.

"You're dividing our forces, John. If they get you, they'll probably get us without too much trouble."

"Sometimes, Ben, you have to have a little trust."

Ben swore under his breath.

"We'll back you, John," Gale said.

"There's plenty of ammunition in those saddlebags, I think. After I fire my rifle, I'm going to leave it here. I figure if I do get in a tangle, I'll have a better chance with the six-gun."

"I don't like it none, John."

"Just do what I ask, Ben. And don't worry about me."

"We will worry," Gale said, and John saw genuine concern in her eyes.

"Keep those rifles hot," John said.

He drew a breath and held it. He took a bead on the bush and slowly squeezed the trigger. The rifle bucked against his shoulder. Smoke and sparks spewed from the barrel. He heard the bullet tear through the brush.

"Nothing there," Ben said in an almost reverent whisper.

Several seconds passed by. John worked the lever and loaded another round into the firing chamber of his rifle.

He fired again, holding slightly lower. The rifle shot sounded like a bullwhip and he heard its echoes resound in the hills.

A figure jumped up, buck naked, dust flowing from his skin like brown water.

"See," John said, "there *was* a jackrabbit behind that bush!"

16

BEN RAISED HIS RIFLE SLIGHTLY, TOOK AIM.

"Don't shoot him," John yelled. "Let him go."

Ben lowered his rifle.

"But he's getting' away."

"Look at him," John said. "He's just a boy."

It was true. The naked brave was small and thin, covered with dirt, but it was obvious that he was no more than twelve years old, if that.

The boy ran over the lip of the mesa and disappeared.

John handed his rifle to Gale.

"Cover me, you two," he said and ran around the pile of rocks. He crouched low and drew his pistol.

"Good luck," Gale called after him.

A Navajo's head bobbed up and Gale fired her rifle. The shot was high, but the brave ducked back down below the ledge.

"Missed him clean," Gale said. "Not by much."

"A miss is as good as a mile," Ben said.

She flashed him a wry smile and Ben's face flushed with embarrassment.

"You really know how to make a woman feel good, Ben Russell," she said.

"Sorry, ma'am. I didn't mean no disrespect."

Mollified, Gale levered another cartridge into the chamber. The spent casing ejected and clanged against the rocks.

John ran in a zigzag pattern toward the laboratory, his feet moving very fast in small, ground-eating steps.

He heard the shots from Gale's rifle and saw the Navajo escape injury. He knew there could be dozens of braves on that long slope up to the mesa. Any one of them could pick him off before he reached the lab. And there could be others just outside the lab, waiting for him.

He reached the back of the building and stopped, breathing hard. He looked back at the line of tailings, the carbon ore glistening in the sun, and could see the dark shapes of Gale's and Ben's heads, the snouts of their rifles. He raised a hand to let them know he was all right. Then he began to slide around to the sidewall of the building. He stepped slow and soft, so as to be almost noiseless.

His temples throbbed with his rapid heartbeat, and something curdled in his stomach, a tangle of nerves that had begun to spark with the first electric shoots of fear. He forced himself to take deep breaths, to quell the rising anxiety he felt at being in a place where he could not see his enemy, a place where the odds were greatly against him. The Navajo were experts at hiding in plain sight. They could be all around him, like black cats at night, ready to spring on him and tear him to bits.

John waited, listening. He counted the seconds in his mind. He heard nothing.

Then he drew his pistol and stepped around the corner of the building, his thumb on the hammer of the Colt.

A great sense of relief coursed through his senses as he looked down the wall toward the door and saw nobody there.

He paced off the steps to the door in his mind. Eight, he figured, if he stretched his stride. He took the first step, waited, then took another. His palm was sweaty on the grip of his pistol, but his thumb held fast to the crosshatched hammer, ready to bear down on it and cock the hammer.

He tried to remember if Gale had closed the lock on the door or left it open. If it was closed, he would have to put a bullet in it to break it open. If not, it would take only a second or two to slip the lock from the door. He had to risk it, either way.

John drew a breath and glanced at the western sky. Far off, puffs of clouds were floating in a phalanx toward the east. If he squinted, they looked like the sails of ships floating across a blue sky. Those clouds might bring weather, he thought, but not soon, not this day. The rest of the sky looked clear and serene.

He took a breath and started running for the door. Anyone below the rim of the mesa-like outcropping might hear him, but if a head popped up, he would be able to get off a shot.

He reached the door.

The lock hung there, open. He slipped it out of the ring and pulled the hasp back. He threw the lock inside the lab and stepped inside. Just as he did, he saw a shadow out of the corner of his eye. He was halfway through the door when he felt a blow to his leg that was still outside. He twisted and saw arms wrapped around his leg. A small Navajo, no more than a boy, had tackled him. But that was the least of his worries, he realized. As he brought the pistol down hard on top of his tackler's head, he saw a grown man with reddish brown skin looming toward him, his arm upraised. In his hand, the Navajo held a large knife poised to strike. The blade flashed in the sun like a fish breaking water on a blue lake.

The Indian boy crumpled under the force of the blow and John kicked at him to knock him away. Just then, before he could slip inside the doorway, the man with the knife reached him before John could bring his pistol to bear.

The young Navajo, senseless, rolled away from the building like a lumpy rug. The Indian with the knife closed on John, his black eyes jittery as bouncing marbles, his scowl ferocious with the flash of his white teeth. John knew the man meant to kill and the muscles in his arms rippled like snakes.

John twisted to meet the charge and swung his pistol toward the hurtling man. The Navajo lashed out with his left hand and grabbed John's right wrist, while his right arm came down like a pendulum with that gleaming knife. John threw up his left hand, grasped the Navajo's wrist, and felt steel cords in the palm of his hand. The Navajo's weight carried him forward like some juggernaut of flesh and John staggered backward through the door, grappling with a man bent on murder.

He could feel the man's animal breath on his face, hot as a desert wind, and he dug his fingernails into the soft flesh of both wrists, feeling the pain in the tips of his fingers. The Navajo made no sound. He did not cry out nor show any signs of the excruciating agony he must have felt. John wrestled the man in a half circle and the two men moved like macabre dancers on a musty stage, John panting from the exertion, the Navajo breathing through his nose like some primitive beast, his mouth half open as if he wanted to slake his thirst on human blood.

The Navajo had a red bandanna tied around his forehead, but wore no war paint. His body reeked of sand and dust and the faint taint of greasewood or creosote, as if he had emerged from the land itself only moments before.

John held on to his pistol with an iron grip even though the Navajo brave was trying his best to wrest it from his hand. Nor could he shake the knife loose from his attacker's hand, no matter how hard he dug his fingers into the man's wrist.

"Voy a matarte, gringo." The Navajo spoke in Spanish. *I'm going to kill you, gringo.*

"No vas a matarme, hoy, Indio," John replied. *You aren't going to kill me today, Indian.*

The two fell to the floor of the laboratory and grappled. The Navajo tried to roll on top of John, but John brought up a knee and drove it into the man's genitals. The brave did not cry out, although John knew the pain must be excruciating.

The two men rolled again, over and over, until they were stopped when the Navajo's back struck an anvil. His body contorted in pain, but he showed no sign of it on his face, nor did he utter anything more than a grunt as the air was knocked out of his lungs.

John struggled to stand, and so did his assailant. The two regained their footing and the Navajo kicked John in the shin. He almost went down, but staggered away, dragging the man with him. They danced in rigid unison, each trying to gain the advantage of the other. They looked like men walking on plates of red-hot iron, their feet rising and falling as first one pushed, then the other.

"You are strong," the Navajo said in Spanish.

"You are strong also," John replied in the same tongue.

"Very brave."

"Like you," John said, winded.

The Navajo grinned for just a second, and a light danced in those black eyes of his as the two men moved around the lab. John was sweating, the Navajo was not.

Sunlight streamed through the windows, columns of light that seemed alive with dust motes that were like tiny golden fireflies. John realized that the fight could go on until one or the other of them weakened and then either he would fire a bullet into the warrior's brain or he would get a knife rammed into his throat. But he could not break the Navajo's hold on his wrists. They were pushing and pulling on each other like men on either end of a crosscut saw. Back and forth, to and fro, they went, each grunting with extra effort, each tiring, but neither willing to quit.

They moved past the door and John kicked it shut. Then he whirled the Navajo around and, with a flick of his elbow, jarred the crossbar loose. It fell into place, locking the two inside the laboratory.

John wondered if there were more Indians outside and, if so, why were they not coming to this one's aid. Were they all converging on Gale and Ben, perhaps flanking them on both sides? No, they couldn't do that without being seen, he decided. But he had his hands full and could not think about that now.

Both men were tiring, but John saw no lessening of the Navajo's strength. He realized that he could not go on much longer. He had to break the Indian's hold on him, end the struggle. He saw only one way to break the deadlock. It meant taking a chance, but taking chances was a part of life. It was, he thought, the undecided man that fell victim to disaster.

John drew in a breath to summon up every ounce of strength he could muster. Then he stopped pushing on the Navajo. He looked the man straight in the eye, fixing him with a look that he hoped would convey both honesty and determination.

"Basta," John shouted into the Navajo's face. *Enough.*

The Navajo's eyes betrayed his surprise. A shadow seemed to crawl across his face. His mouth went slack and his upper lip sagged downward to cover his teeth.

Then John released his grip on the wrist that held the knife. At the same time, he jerked his gun hand with a mighty wrench of his arm. He felt the Navajo's fingers loosen. He ducked down and scrabbled backward, keeping his feet evenly spaced in a squatting position.

The Navajo swung the knife, slicing the air over John's head. This threw the Navajo off balance and he staggered away in a half turn. John stayed where he was and balled his left hand into a fist. He swung hard and drove his fist into the Navajo's back with such force he could feel the electricity shoot up his arm. His hand went numb. But the blow rocked the Navajo off his feet and he fell to his knees. John rose up and grabbed the hand that held the knife. He bent it backward until he heard the bone snap. The knife tumbled to the floor.

John swung the pistol hard at the side of the warrior's head, butt-first, and smashed the Indian in the temple. He heard a small cracking sound and the Navajo's head snapped to one side and he crumpled as if all the bones in his body had melted. He fell to one side and lay still, his eyes closed, his breathing shallow.

John stepped over the fallen man and aimed the pistol at a point in the center of the Navajo's forehead.

He cocked the Colt and drew another breath, held it.

Then his finger curled around the trigger in the attack position.

The Navajo was a scant second away from eternity and the laboratory went deathly still.

17

BEN PULLED A BANDANNA FROM HIS HIND POCKET AND DABBED AT the sweat beaded up on his forehead. He wiped his hands on his trousers and put the bandanna back in his pocket. He looked longingly at the approaching puff clouds wafting like clumps of cotton in the western sky. He wished they would cover the sun, but they were still far off, and the disk in the sky was a blazing furnace. John had slipped around the corner of the laboratory building a good ten or fifteen minutes ago, and neither he nor Gale had seen any smoke rising from the chimney. Neither had spoken to the other in all that time, and it was so quiet it seemed to Ben that they were both shouting at each other in the silence of their minds.

"You reckon . . ."

"Ben, I . . ."

They both spoke at once and then both laughed.

"It's just so quiet," she said, "and no smoke from that chimney yonder. I do hope nothing's happened to John."

"As long as we haven't heard a shot, John's probably all right."

"Then why hasn't he stoked up the danged stove in that lab?"

"I don't know," Ben said, wrinkling his forehead in puzzlement. "Maybe he's still outside, lookin' things over."

"It's mighty peculiar," she said. "And would you look at them clouds a-floatin' in from the northwest. That means weather in my book."

"Later, maybe. I just wish them clouds would cover the sun for a little while."

"Take a pull on one of them canteens, Ben. It might cool you down."

"Water's near to boilin' in the one I got here," he said.

They were quiet for a few more minutes. Fidgety. Then something to the north caught Ben's eye. Way down on the plain. A puff of dust, he thought, and he kept his gaze on it for a few more seconds.

"Gale, looky yonder, toward Tucson. You see anything?"

Gale scanned the valley below.

"Could be the start of a dust devil," she said. "Hard to tell."

"Yeah. You see the dust, though, right?"

"I see some dust," she said.

"Could be more Navajos riding up here," Ben said.

"That would not be good. We're probably outnumbered as it is."

"How many Navajos are running around this part of the country?"

Gale shrugged. "I don't know. Kit Carson chased most of 'em to reservations, but many of 'em didn't like it and broke loose. No tellin' how many are runnin' loose."

The dust seemed to subside and Ben let out a sigh of relief.

The two were silent for several seconds, both staring toward the northwest.

"Ben?" Gale said.

"Yeah?"

"You and John," she said, "You got any ties anywheres else?"

Ben shook his head. "Nope."

"No family?"

"John lost his ma and pa and little sister in Colorado. Neither of us has any close kin. Why?"

"Oh, I'm just thinkin', that's all."

Ben let out a long breath through his nose.

"You got somethin' in mind, Gale?"

"Maybe. Not right away. I just wanted to know. I like both of you. A lot."

Ben blushed slightly.

"That's mighty nice of you to say, ma'am."

"You're good folks," she said.

Ben sat up straight peering over the pile of tailings. There was dust in the sky. He could not tell if it was windblown or caused by cattle, sheep, or horses. But there was too much dust to ignore.

"I see it," Gale said. "Looks like riders, maybe, comin' our way. See those dark specks every now and then? Inside the dust cloud."

"I see somethin'," Ben said. "Can't make it out."

"Could be Injuns," she said. "They don't seem to be ridin' real fast if they are."

Whatever was kicking up the dust was too far away for Ben to tell what it was. He felt a trickle of sweat course down his temple and his gut tightened. The wind was blowing their way, and so was the dust.

"Don't you have a spyglass?" Gale asked. "My heart's squeezed so tight I can hardly breathe wondering who in tarnation is kicking up all that dust."

"Yeah, John has a pair of field glasses in his saddlebags. Wonder why I didn't think of it."

"I'll get 'em," Gale said and leaned her rifle against the pilings. She dragged one set of saddlebags toward her. They were heavy. She opened one and began rummaging through it with both hands. "Not in this one," she said. She dipped her hands into the other one, her fingers probing for a large object that could be a pair of binoculars in a leather case.

Ben shaded his eyes and peered intently at the cloud of dust. He could just make out the legs, chest, and head of a horse in the forefront of the dust, but could not make out the rider.

"Ah, here they are," Gale said, pulling the case out of John's saddlebag. She took out the binoculars and put them to her eyes. She adjusted the focus.

"I can just make out part of a horse," she said to Ben.

"Give 'em here," he said. "Let me take a gander."

Gale scooted over close to Ben and handed him the binoculars. She leaned back and got her rifle, but stayed close to him as if she did not want to return to her former position.

Ben refocused the field glasses and gazed down in the sunlit valley. The glasses magnified his view by a factor of twenty and he could make out the lead horse. The rider was still obscured by the blowing dust, but the horse looked to be a fine mount.

"That ain't no Injun pony up front," he said.

"The Navajos ride everything from burros to saddle horses," Gale said.

"It's a tall horse, I think, maybe sixteen hands high. Can't make out the rider."

Just then, they both heard a quail call. It was very loud and close at hand. The sound seemed to be coming from over the rim of the mesa.

The sound startled Ben and he lowered the binoculars.

The call persisted.

"That ain't no quail," Gale said.

"Sounds like one. What is it?"

"Navajos imitate 'em. It's some kind of signal, I reckon, from down below the mesa."

Ben felt the skin tighten on the back of his neck. He peered over at the laboratory, all along the edge of the mesa, then on both sides.

"Somethin's up, maybe," he said. "But I don't see nothin'."

Gale scanned the same area, her finger curled around the trigger of her rifle.

The calling stopped, and they could both hear the wind crooning in the valley. It sounded like a faraway river or some creature keening just beyond their view.

He looked up at the sky. The little clouds were even closer, but behind them huge altocumulus clouds were forming, giant billowing thunderheads as white as snow.

"Hear that wind?" he said. "And see them clouds yonder?"

"Yes," she said. "There'll be a storm likely. We get 'em here. That wind. It means we'll get a cloudburst come evenin'."

"Well, we got the cave and that lab if John takes it over. We can stay dry."

Gale didn't say anything. She was looking at the dust cloud again.

"Take another look at what's down there," she said. "Looks to be a passel of riders."

Ben put the binoculars back up to his eyes. The riders were still miles away, but he could now see the lead rider better. His throat lumped up as he saw the column behind him. And he thought he saw something fluttering above them, like a kerchief or some kind of flapping bird.

The lead rider was dressed in blue. But he saw a yellow stripe down his leg. Behind him, the next rider held a staff and the flying thing was flapping over his head.

"Them riders might be soldiers," he said. "I think I see a guidon. And they're ridin' two by two. Injuns don't ride that way, do they?"

"No," she said. "Let me take a look."

Ben handed Gale the field glasses.

"I believe those are soldiers," she said. "Yes, I can see their uniforms. United States Cavalry, Ben. And they're probably tracking those Navajo jaybirds hunkered down below this mesa."

"You sure?" he said.

"Pretty sure. Still a lot of dust a-blowin', but they're riding in formation and they got them yellow-striped pants. Might have come from Tucson out of Fort Apache."

"Let's hope they're chasin' them Navajos we got camped on our doorstep."

"Well, if John ever sends smoke up that chimney, they

might see it and come ridin' this way. That'll sure drive off them Injuns."

But there was no sign of smoke from the lab's chimney and the quail calling had begun again, loud and piercing, from two or more Navajo throats.

"Damn," Ben said. "Maybe I better go down there and see what's happened to Johnny. It's been too long."

He started to rise and Gale put a hand on his arm.

"You stay right here, Ben," she said. "I don't want to be left here all by my lonesome."

"But John . . ."

"John Savage looks like a man who can take care of himself. If the Navajos had killed him, they'd be all over us like a nest of hornets."

Ben sank back down.

The piping calls stopped and there was a silence once again.

"I wonder what it means," Ben muttered.

"What?"

"All that callin'."

"Probably a warning," she said.

"Warning who?"

Gale didn't answer. She didn't like it. The Navajos were talking to one another about something. And whatever it was, it wasn't good for them or for John Savage.

She tensed up, drew a breath, and held it. She felt as if something was going to happen at any minute.

Something terrible.

She thought of John and wondered why he hadn't gotten inside the lab. Was he dead? He might be lying on the other side of the building, his throat cut, his head scalped down to raw meat. She shuddered at the thought.

The clouds were rolling in and the wind was picking up. It blew at her hat and hair and whistled in the rocks on the mountainside and the pile of tailings.

She bit her lip and tightened her grip on the stock of her rifle.

She was trying her best not to scream.

18

———◆———

JOHN'S HEART SEEMED TO STOP IN HIS CHEST. IT WAS ONLY HIS breathing that had stopped, but he felt as if time had ceased to be in that instant of decision. He looked down at the pistol in his hand, wondering if it carried a curse. He was so close to killing a man. All it would take would be a tick of his trigger finger and the Navajo would be rubbed off the page of life forever.

The pistol weighed heavy in his hand. The grip burned through his palm as if it was on fire. His trigger finger stiffened and froze as if paralyzed. He looked at the face of the Navajo. The Indian's eyes were closed, his mouth partially opened, the fierceness in his visage vanished. He was a young man, no more than fifteen or sixteen, John figured. Nearly his own age. Could he kill such a man so easily? Could he shorten a life with a simple pull of the trigger? He could, but something in him rebelled against his own ferocious instinct.

The two had fought, each trying to kill the other in the heat of combat. But now, there was a winner and a loser. Was chivalry a thing of the distant past, forgotten in a modern age where the pistol replaced the sword and the lance? Did a man lose all compassion when his blood ran hot? Did the power to kill mean a man had to kill?

His father's words came back to him in those fateful seconds.

"When you take a man's life, son," Dan Savage had said to him one day when they were hunting deer high in the Rockies, *"you'd better have a damned good reason. And if you kill a man for no good reason, you kill part of your own soul. You don't just kill the man, you kill yourself. You kill what made you a man in the first place."*

He had killed men, that was true. But he had had good reason. Those men had done him harm, had murdered his family. What had this Navajo done? He had fought, and fought bravely. He had tried to kill a white man, his natural enemy, but he hadn't succeeded. Did that justify killing him? Maybe. At that moment, John did not know. He stood on the edge of a high cliff, the wind blowing at his back. If he fired his pistol, the wind would blow him off and he would plunge a thousand feet into an abyss. He would live with that Navajo's sleeping face in his thoughts and dreams for the rest of his life.

His father's message was written on the barrel of the pistol in his hand. Written in Spanish. But he knew its meaning and his father's words came back to him now, in English. *Neither draw me without reason, nor keep me without honor.*

John eased the hammer back down to half cock and stepped away from the unconscious Navajo. He looked around the room for a piece of rope. There were plenty of ropes here and there. He found a piece of manila rope that was the right length. He holstered his pistol and picked up the rope, carrying it to the fallen man. He knelt down, turned the man over, and tied his wrists together behind his back. He picked up the man's knife and stuck it in his belt. It was a large imitation of a bowie knife, with sharp edges on both sides of the blade, a brass guard, and an antler handle that was worn down to the outlines of the ridges.

He dragged the man to the wall and propped him up in a

sitting position near the stove. There was a welt on the man's temple and it was swelling to the size of a darning egg. Satisfied, John put sticks of kindling in the stove, stacked them in the shape of a pyramid. He found wood chips and scattered those beneath the sticks of wood. He struck a match, held the flame to a pair of chips until they caught fire. He dropped the match onto the other chips and gently fanned the flame until it spread. As soon as the kindling caught, he closed the door and made sure the damper was open.

"You, white man. Why you tie me?"

"You speak English," John said.

"I speak."

"Are you Red Hand?"

The man shook his head.

"I am called Coyote."

"My name is John. John Savage."

"You do not kill me."

"No. I have no reason."

"I kill you, John Savage."

"You didn't."

Coyote smiled.

"You tie me," he said. "You kill now?"

"Not if you tell me why you tried to kill me."

"Red Hand say kill."

"Why?"

"White man bad."

"We mean you no harm, Coyote."

"You shoot. You want kill boy."

"You know why we shot at that boy. He was trying to kill us."

Coyote smiled again. He nodded. "That is true," he said.

He struggled with his bonds and John shook a finger at him.

"Don't try to get away, Coyote. Or I will shoot you."

"Coyote no run."

"How many Navajos are with you? Tell me the truth now."

"Three."

"Just three?"

"Red Hand come when sun go to sleep. He say take the horses of the white man."

"So there's just you, that boy, and one other. Is that right?"

"Three only. We wait for Red Hand."

"Where is Red Hand?"

"He go. Not know where."

John was relieved to know that they were not outnumbered. But there were still two Navajos outside. He wondered why they hadn't come after Coyote. Maybe they were ordered to stay put. A boy and probably another man. Now he had a prisoner and didn't know what to do with him. Coyote spoke only a little English. Perhaps he could find out more if he spoke Spanish. But his Spanish was not perfect. There were a lot of words he didn't know. Still, he might be able to find out how many men were with Red Hand. If he was returning at sunset, they'd have to get away or risk a bloody fight with the Navajos.

John tended to the fire. He made sure it was smoky, and added more kindling. He closed the damper for a few seconds on the chimney, then opened it. Gale and Ben ought to be able to see more than one puff of smoke.

"Will the two men outside come after you, Coyote?" John closed the door to the stove and walked over to his prisoner.

"They will wait for Mano Rojo."

"You cannot stay in the mine anymore."

"No?"

"No. I am trying to catch a bad white man and I need the mine. Will you and Mano Rojo go away and leave us alone?"

"You tell Mano Rojo."

"Will he listen?"

"He will listen."

"Will you tell him if I let you go?"

"I will tell him."

John didn't know if he could trust Coyote. He would be taking a big chance if he let his prisoner go. Now he held the advantage.

"How many men with Red Hand?" John asked.

"Two more."

"Is that all?"

"Yes. No more. We are few. We are hungry. We live like the rabbit. We hide. We look for food. We hide."

John was getting a picture of the life these runaway Navajos were leading. They were refugees from some Indian reservation, wanting to live free but having no means. And they were probably being hunted by the U.S. Army. Or, worse, by a posse of civilians who would probably shoot the Navajos on sight.

A pounding on the door interrupted John's thoughts.

"John, open up. It's me, Ben."

John walked to the door, lifted the latch. Gale and Ben rushed inside the lab. John closed the door, then dropped the latch. Both were breathless; neither saw Coyote at first. They were still adjusting their eyes to the dim light in the lab.

"You took your sweet time, Johnny," Ben said, "lettin' us in."

"I was busy."

"Now, now, boys," Gale said, "let's not quarrel. John, there's a small troop of soldiers ridin' this way. Maybe a dozen."

"A patrol?" John said.

"Looks like," Ben told him. "That's why we ran down here. They're headin' straight for us. Them Navajos light a shuck?"

John hiked a thumb toward Coyote.

Ben looked over at the wall. Gale twisted her head in that same direction.

"You got one," Ben exclaimed.

The three walked over to Coyote.

"Recognize him, Gale?" John said. "He's one of Red Hand's band."

She shook her head.

"Nope, never seen this one before. Where's the others? Where's that young 'un you run off?"

"There are two more," John said. "Waiting for Red Hand and this one."

"Where are they?" Ben asked. "You got 'em tied up outside?"

John shook his head. "No, they're probably running from the soldiers by now. This one calls himself Coyote."

"Well, he sure looks moth-eaten," Ben said.

John noticed Coyote's ragged clothing for the first time. He had been studying his face, a face that was hard to decipher, round and dark, with a small pinched nose, sensuous lips, high prominent cheekbones, black hair. His shirt was thin and threadbare, a pale blue, as if it had been washed out in lye soap a thousand times. His sash was faded black, the thread unraveling in several places. His pants were old, too, grimy and dusty, tan, and his moccasins were without beads or ornaments, just scuffed and patched and holey.

"Bedraggled as hell," Gale said.

"He speaks a little English and some Spanish," John said.

"What're you goin' to do with him, John?" Ben asked.

"I don't know."

"How'd you get him?" Gale asked.

"He came after me with this knife." John pointed to the knife in his belt. "I knocked him cold with the barrel of my Colt."

Gale and Ben looked at each other.

Both were silent for a few seconds.

"You tie him up real good?" Ben said, a trace of trepidation in his voice.

"Good enough," John said.

"I think the soldiers saw your smoke, John," Gale said. "They turned right afterward. They might have seen us run down here from behind those tailings. If they were lookin' through their glasses."

"Well, let's go out and wave them up here," John said.

"What about him—Coyote there?" Ben asked.

"He'll keep," John said. "I don't want the soldiers to get him."

"You don't?" Gale said. "Why not?"

"I think we might make a friend out of him."

"Friends with a Navajo renegade? I don't think so."

"Ever try?" John asked.

Gale looked at him with flinty eyes, her head cocked like a bird eying a bug.

"They don't tame," she said, and John detected the bitterness in her voice. "I was brought up knowin' the only good Injun was a dead Injun."

"Maybe that ought to change," John said.

He lifted the crossbar and opened the door. The three of them stepped out into the sunlight.

Gale and Ben held their rifles at the ready as they walked to the edge of the flat and gazed down at the approaching soldiers. There was no sign of the other two Navajos. They seemed to have vanished among the rocks. John wondered if they had horses or were on foot.

"They've broken up," Ben said. "About half of them are ridin' south."

It was true. Six soldiers were just now climbing the road up the slope toward the laboratory. Seven others were probing to the south, guidon flying. The wind blew at their faces and John saw the giant thunderheads floating toward them. The small clouds were gone from the sky, swallowed up by the big white ones.

"They're hunting the other two," John said, a trace of sadness in his voice.

"Good riddance, I say," Gale said.

John wished he had the other two inside the lab. He felt sorry for the two that got away. He felt sorry for Coyote. The Navajos were being hunted down like animals. Kept like animals on reservations. Prisons. It didn't seem right. They were people, human beings like himself.

"I hope they get away," he said softly.

And Gale glared at him, her lips pursed tight. The hatred in her went deep, he thought. But then, a Navajo had killed her husband.

Red Hand.

It was too bad that one bad apple had to ruin the barrel, he thought.

19

THE ARMY LIEUTENANT HELD A GLOVED HAND UP TO SIGNAL A HALT upon reaching the top of the shelf.

"Sergeant Pierson," he said, "post two sentries at our flanks."

"Yes, sir," Pierson said and ordered two men to take up positions on either side of the dwindling column.

John could see the look of distaste on the sergeant's face, but the young lieutenant was unaware of the older man's feelings about the asinine order.

"Hello," Gale said. "What brings the army out this way?"

The lieutenant rode up on top of the shelf, leaving his men behind on the slope. He was a trim, slight man, with neatly cut hair, sideburns, a wire-thin moustache. His uniform was covered with dust, which he patted with a gloved hand.

"Ma'am, I'm Second Lieutenant Clive Bellaugh," he said, "and we're looking for some bandits."

"Bandits?" Gale said.

"Yes, ma'am. You see any ride this way?"

"Why, no, officer. There's just the three of us. I'm Gale Gill and I'm the owner of this mine." She cocked a thumb and pointed to the adit, which the lieutenant could plainly see from where he sat his horse.

"What kind of mine?" Bellaugh asked.

"Gold," she said.

"Well, you'd better be careful, ma'am. There was a gold mine robbed yesterday south of Tucson. Every man jack of them killed except one, who escaped to tell us about it. He was badly wounded, but he might pull through."

"Why, that's awful, Lieutenant," Gale said. "Do you know who the robbers were?"

"We have a couple of names. First, though, I'd like to know who these two gentlemen with you are."

"I'm John Savage," John said.

"And I'm Ben Russell."

The lieutenant moved his lips, saying the names to himself.

"Anybody else here working the mine?" Bellaugh said.

Gale shook her head.

"Just us three," she said. "We're not working it yet. It was my husband's, and he was killed. But there's gold in it and we're going to get it out. We were just looking it over, kind of figuring out what to do."

"Yes'm. I guess we'll be on our way, then."

"What about the robbers? You said you might know who they are?"

"The man who got away said he heard two of the names, maybe three. He was in pretty bad shape. But he was pretty sure one of the men was called Cruddy and the other one was named Harley or Arlie, something like that."

John stiffened slightly at the mention of the names, but he didn't betray the flash of recognition that burst through his mind. Ben swallowed hard, but kept silent.

"Names don't ring a bell with me," Gale said quickly. "Hope you catch 'em."

John thought that the soldiers would leave then, but the lieutenant didn't move. He seemed eager to talk.

"It's not only white men we're after, Mrs. Gill. This fellow who got away said they saw some Navajos skulking around the mine. One of them shot his partner and the others came after them with rifles. It was a kind of trap, we think. Because once they all left the mine, the white men were waiting in ambush, started gunning them down."

"Did they get any gold?" Gale asked.

"They got some bars that had been smelted in Tucson. Worth a heap of money, the man said."

"Maybe they should have kept those bars in a bank," she said.

"People around here don't trust banks too much."

"Too bad," she said.

"Well, ma'am, we'll be on our way. You see anything suspicious, you come to Tucson, report it to the sheriff. He'll get word to me."

"I surely will, Lieutenant. Good-bye."

"Good-bye, ma'am."

The lieutenant turned his horse and rode down to his men. He said something and they all moved out. The two flankers fell in behind the column, which headed down the slope single file.

Gale waited until the soldiers were out of earshot before she spoke.

"You hear what he said, John? About Harley or Arlie?"

"Ollie," John said.

Ben nodded. "Sure as shootin' that was Ollie Hobart."

"You know the other name he mentioned?" she said. "Cruddy, wasn't it?"

"We do," John said. "He's one of Ollie's men."

"I should have asked who the miners were," she said. "But I probably didn't know them. Neither Clarence nor I knew any hard-rock miners around here."

"If that was Ollie," Ben said, "he won't be satisfied with what gold he got. 'Pears to me, he might be interested in your mine, Gale, once we salt it and get the word out we struck gold."

"You'd think he'd be satisfied and go somewheres else," she said.

"We'll have to work fast," John said. "Make sure he

doesn't leave Tucson or wherever he's holed up. The sooner we salt this mine and take that ore into the assay office in Tucson, the sooner we can lay our trap for Ollie Hobart."

"What about that Injun in there?" she said. "What are you going to do with him?"

"Let's talk to him," John said. "Maybe those Navajos who were with Hobart were part of his band."

"Will he talk?" Ben asked.

"He might talk," Gale said, "but will he tell us the truth?"

The three of them stood there watching the soldiers descend the slope. On the plain, the column turned left and headed south, still in single file. They watched the soldiers until they dwindled to small black dots and disappeared in the cloud shadows of the desert.

"Let's get to that Injun of yours, John," Gale said and turned toward the door of the lab.

She entered first, followed by Ben and John.

They all had to adjust their eyes to the dim light after being in the sun.

A shaft of light from one of the side windows jiggled with gelatinous light. Dust motes fluttered like gilded fireflies. The side window on the opposite wall blared with sunlight that was weak and shapeless, seemingly trapped in shadow.

John glanced at the place where he had left Coyote tied up, a few feet from the open window.

Coyote was gone.

John raced to the spot where Coyote had squatted, saw the piece of rope lying like a dead albino snake. He walked to the window and looked out onto the empty mesa. He could hear the wind moaning through the eaves, saw dust slide across the flat earth, appear and reappear in the blotches of cloud shadows that clotted the landscape.

"What the hell, Johnny?" Ben said.

"Your Injun run off, did he?" Gale asked.

"He's not my Indian," John said. "And yes, he got away. Must have worked the rope loose while we were outside."

"So now we've got us a Injun prowlin' around some-wheres," Ben said.

"He's long gone, I'm sure," John said, turning away from the window. "Maybe we'd better go, too. I want to go back and get that chunk of ore, Gale, and then salt that mine."

Gale frowned.

"We'd better check on our horses, anyway," she said. "I wouldn't put it past that thievin' redskin to make off with 'em."

"They were still there when we came in here," Ben said.

"Yes," Gale said, "but that Injun's escaped and he might want to ride instead of walk. John, you should have killed that murderin' skunk when you had the chance."

John said nothing, but strode to the door. Gale and Ben came out.

"I'd better lock this," Gale said. "Where's the lock?"

"Inside," John said.

She found the lock, closed the door, and put the lock back on, closed it, and pulled on it to make sure the bolt had caught. Ben was already walking toward their horses.

"Here's the key, John," Gale said, handing it to him. "I won't be comin' back with you. Not with all those Navajos running about. I sure wish you had shot that Coyote. The only good Injun . . ."

"Yeah, I know. He was a man, Gale. Unarmed. I have his knife right here inside my belt. Right now he's harmless, probably running like a scared jackrabbit."

"Or waitin' to foller us to the ranch."

"I guess if you like to worry, that one's as good as any."

"What are you, John? An Injun lover?"

"Not particularly. But I talked to the man. I could have killed him, yes. It just didn't seem right."

"Seem right? He was tryin' to kill you, wasn't he?"

"I reckon."

"There's your answer," she said. The two started walking toward the mine. "With Injuns, it's kill or be killed."

"Not this time," he said.

"What do you mean 'not this time'?"

"This time, I won. He lost. I think he might have become a friend. In time."

Gale snorted.

"A friend? More like a sworn enemy. The minute you turn your back on one of them redskins, they want to lift your scalp."

"I have to try," John said. "My pa always said if you could make a friend out of an enemy, you got a good mark in the Lord's book."

"Oh, he said that, did he? Well, you're not going to try and make a friend out of Oliver Hobart, are you? If so, I'll keep that chunk of ore and you and Ben can just ride on to Tucson and shake hands with the enemy."

"Gale, I can't explain it. Just let it drop, will you?"

"Sure, I'll let it drop, John Savage. Just mark my words. That Injun's goin' to remember you and first chance he gets . . ." She made a cutting sound and drew a finger across her throat.

Ben was already mounted up when Gale and John took the reins of their horses from him.

"I put your rifle back in its scabbard," Ben said. "At least that Injun didn't get that."

"Yeah," John said, conscious of the withering glare from Gale as he climbed into the saddle.

They rode off the mesa and down the long slope back to the road. The sky filled with clouds, their white bellies turning dark as soot. In the distance they heard the rumble of thunder and by the time they turned toward Gale's sheep ranch, they could see jagged streaks of lightning lacing the black clouds to the west. The horses were nervous and jittery. Gent seemed to jump underneath the saddle every time a roll of thunder pealed across the heavens.

John thought of Coyote, wondering how he would fare in the storm. He was no Indian lover, he told himself, but he still had the feeling that he and the Navajo could have been friends. More than that, he wondered how he would feel now if he had pulled that trigger and sent the man scampering through the valley of death. It would have been easy. Just to pull that trigger.

That was the trouble. The trouble with the six-gun hanging from his belt. It wasn't cursed, he was sure.

But it had gotten a mite too easy to kill a man with that pistol.

Way too easy.

20

THERE WAS NO SUNSET THAT DAY. THE SKIES HAD DARKENED WITH black elephantine clouds by the time Gale, Ben, and John reached the sheep ranch. Thunder boomed in the distance and lightning streaked the far sky, stippling the clouds with vibrant latticework that looked like liquid silver. Ben and John helped the herders get the sheep into barns and by the time they were finished, the winds were blowing grass and sticks across the fields and slamming into Gale's house with a lashing fury that rattled the shutters and keened a banshee wail in the eaves.

Gale lit the lamps in the front room and the kitchen as Ben and John stood in the dim light, watching her move like a wraith, her snowy hair flowing like a white cloud above the floor.

"You boys set down," she said. "There, on the divan."

She left the room as the two men sat down. They heard her footsteps as she went into the kitchen. Gusts of wind pounded at the door, rattled the windows, and made the windmill outside change pitch and sing a whirring melody.

Gale poured whiskey into stout glass tumblers and barred

the front door. Lightning flashes glazed the windows and thunder made the house shudder with every loud crash.

"In my wildest dreams," Ben said, "I never thought I'd wind up as a sheepherder."

Gale laughed.

"You didn't herd those sheep, Ben, the dogs did."

"Yah, that's true," Ben said. "What kind of dogs were those, anyway?"

"They're Border collies," Gale said. "Bred to tend and herd sheep."

"I never saw a dog work that hard," Ben said.

They had eaten from their saddlebags on the ride back and now they drank the whiskey and watched the lightning flicker on the windowpanes and listened to the rumbling thunder. It had not yet rained.

"Back there, when the thunder started," John said, "and that lightning crackled, I thought I heard gunshots. Either of you hear it?"

"Must be your imagination," Ben said, smacking his lips and licking off the spilled whiskey.

"Come to think of it," Gale said, "a couple of those lightning cracks did sound a lot like rifle shots."

"That ain't nothin'," Ben said. "Most of 'em do sound like rifle shots."

"I don't know," John said. "It gets a man to thinking."

He was thinking about those soldiers and Hobart. But he was also thinking about Red Hand and the Navajos. If they were in cahoots with Ollie, a cold-blooded killer, he couldn't think of a more diabolical and vicious collection of murderers. If Lieutenant Bellaugh had been ambushed by such a force, he would have had a fight on his hands. He hoped those weren't gunshots he'd heard, but if they were, he hoped Bellaugh and the soldiers were victorious and had Hobart slung across a saddle, dead, or in irons.

"A penny," Gale said to John.

"Huh?"

"For your thoughts," she said.

He told her what he had been thinking. She waved a hand in the air.

"Why worry about something you can't do anything about?" she said. "You and Ben have your work cut out for you in the next several days."

"I know," John said. "Tomorrow, we'll take that ore sample with us to the mine. Ben and I will do some lab work on some of those tailings, put them in the mine, then take the ore to the assay office in Tucson and wait for the test results."

"Then what?" Gale asked.

"Oh, we'll brag about our mine and let word get out to Hobart."

"Then we'll wait," Ben said. "Just the two of us." There was more than a trace of wry sarcasm in his voice. He looked gloomy, John thought. Gloomy as a kicked dog.

"That's something we'll have to work out," John said and took another swallow of whiskey. He wasn't a drinking man, but it had turned cold outside when they were rounding up the sheep and the whiskey warmed him, felt good in his belly. Ben held his glass out for another drink and Gale poured his glass full. She sipped at hers but offered more to John, who shook his head.

"Clarence liked his whiskey," she said, dreamy-eyed. "So I learned to tolerate it. But if I take a drink twice a year, that's enough for me. Tonight doesn't count."

The wind raged outside like some snarling beast. It sniffed at the cracks and crevices in the house, bolted in through small openings, carried a chill with it.

"I think I'll light a fire," Gale said. "This is turning into a real blue norther."

"I'll help you," Ben said. He got up and walked to the fireplace, bent down, and began stacking kindling on the grate. Gale opened the damper in the brick chimney, took a taper from the mantel, struck it on the hearth, and lit the dry wood. Flames licked the kindling and the wood crackled like a thousand crickets, the released gases whispering and hissing like snakes.

Ben added logs to the kindling and the heat from the fire began to warm the chilly room.

"I'll get you that ore sample, John," Gale said when the fire was blazing. "You might want to leave early in the morning."

"I do," John said. "Think this rainstorm will blow over tonight?"

"Hard to tell," she said. "Most do. You might have to watch out for flash floods. The way that wind is a-blowin', the storm might just whip on by in a hurry."

She left the room and returned a few minutes later with a wooden box. It had a lid. She set it down in front of John and then sat in the chair opposite the divan. John opened the box and took out the rock.

Ben whistled as John turned the ore over in his hands so that they could see all sides of it.

Bands of gold were threaded through the rock. They saw specks of mica and quartz, but the gold veins gleamed in the firelight.

"The ore is rich," Ben said. "We never found ore like this out in Colorado. Chunks and specks, sure, but not veined gold like this. That mine of your'n ought to be worked."

"I just couldn't go there after Clarence died," Gale said. "I knew he was in that mine and I knew I would feel his presence. I—I just wanted to cherish it as a kind of shrine, I suppose. Something left in his memory."

"I understand," John said. "I couldn't go back to our mine, either. My father's spirit is still there. My mother's and my sister's, too."

Ben and John returned to the divan. John set the ore on the table next to their drink glasses. The rock seemed to pulse with energy. It caught the lamplight and the firelight and seemed to glow with a powerful energy.

"You poor boy," Gale said. "I—I mean, I know you're not a boy, but losing your whole family like that."

"You don't mind us using the mine to catch Hobart, Gale?" John asked.

She sighed.

"You know, I've thought about it a lot since we were up

there. When—when we went inside, I could almost feel Clarence's presence. I kept thinking we'd see him at the end of that shaft."

John nodded.

"When my father died," he said, "I felt that presence. Very strong. When Ben and I found the pistol he had given me, and the gold that was cached away, I felt my father's spirit, I guess you'd call it. It was in the mountain air, in the stream, in the very air we breathed. I almost felt that if I closed my eyes and then opened them, I'd see him squatting by the creek, panning gold, or working one of the rockers, or swinging a pick up in the mine."

Ben cleared his throat.

"I—I reckon I must have felt the same way, Johnny. I never told you because I was so choked up and seein' everybody dead, I just couldn't say what was in my mind. But I felt them all there, somehow, lookin' at us, pinin' for us, and it seemed like I could hear them whisperin' on the breeze that blew along that creek. Ever' last one of 'em."

Gale let out a breath as if she had held it pent up in her chest for a very long time.

Then they heard the first spatters of rain, like shot thrown against the walls of the house, against the shutters and the panes of glass. They all listened to it and stared at the fire in the fireplace and became still as if each was feeling some personal presence and as if the wind that flung the rain was full of whispers, whispers from the dead each had lost.

Thunder boomed close at hand and lightning smeared a silver sheen on the windows, brief but vivid, the light vanishing like ghostly apparitions and leaving an afterimage on their retinas.

"Here it comes," Gale said.

"Yep, there's the rain," Ben said and took another swallow of whiskey.

John held up a hand.

"Listen," he said.

Echoes of the last thunderclap reverberated across the

skies. The rain pattered on the windows, soft except when gusts blasted the drops.

"Just thunder," Gale said.

"No, underneath. I hear something."

They all listened. The spatter of rain against the glass windows, the small thuds of the drops against the outer walls. The sob of the wind in the eaves.

"There," John said. "Hear it?"

"I don't hear nothin' but rain and wind," Ben said.

"I—I might have heard something," Gale said. "Can't quite make it out."

"Someone's calling," John said. "Far off."

Gale got up and walked to the front window. She looked out, then pressed her ear against the glass.

"I hear it now," she said. "Someone is calling. Maybe the sheep . . ."

John and Ben joined her at the front window. They could all hear someone yelling.

"Help," Ben said. "It sounds like help."

"It sure does to me," John said.

"I think you're right," Gale said. "Don't sound like none of my hands, neither."

John went to the door and opened it.

He heard the sound of hoofbeats, very faint, but distinguishable in between gusts of wind and the splash of rain. He stepped out of the light and stood peering into the darkness.

He saw them then, two riders, their horses sloshing through puddles of water, throwing up a silvery spray.

"Somebody's coming," he called into the house.

"I can't see 'em," Gale said.

"How many?" Ben asked, still standing at the window with Gale.

"Looks like two. Can't make them out," John said.

"Help, help," one of the riders called and his voice was snatched away by a gust of wind. But they could all hear it, and then a ripping spear of lightning cracked through a cloud, splintering into a dozen branches. The light lit up the fields and illumined the two riders, freezing them in brilliance for a split second. Then the thunder drowned out all sound, even the rain.

John waved at the riders, hoping they could see him. That was an American voice, he knew, and whoever called was in trouble.

"Over here," John shouted, but it was like yelling into a vacuum, into the rolling thunder. Yet the riders came on, galloping through grass and puddles of water. They appeared to be in slow motion, slowed by the weariness of their mounts and the curtains of rain, the blowing wind.

Gale and Ben rushed outside and stood beside John.

"Who is it?" Gale asked.

"I don't know," John said. "But they're hurting for sure."

The riders came into view, two silhouettes, faces dark, unidentifiable.

But John saw the yellow stripes on their trousers and the gleam of brass as another sheet of lightning burst light over a wide area.

"Soldiers," Gale breathed.

Thirty yards away, John saw one of the horses stumble. The man riding it was bent over the saddle horn. The man in the lead held up a hand. He looked worn out, weary beyond caring, his uniform black as sin, plastered to his body with wetness.

"It's that lieutenant," John said. "Bellaugh. And one of his men."

The horses came to an abrupt halt a few feet from where the three people were standing.

The slumped-over rider slid from the saddle and fell hard onto the wet ground, sending up a splash of water.

"Help us," Bellaugh said, dropping his hand.

He crumpled then, and John saw him go limp. His right sleeve dripped blood and his face was ashen.

The cloudburst hit as he and Ben rushed out to grab Bellaugh before he fell from his horse. Gale ran to the fallen soldier, sloshing through ankle-high water.

The rain fell with a drenching fury, all at once, as if the whole sky had opened, emptying out an enormous black well.

21

THREE OF THE SHEEPHERDERS CAME RUNNING OUT OF THE BUNK-
house, wearing slickers. They spoke in rapid Spanish to each
other. One of the army horses snorted as a gust of wind rattled its bridle. Rain stung John's eyes as he swung Bellaugh
around to get a better grip on his waist.

Gale took charge.

"Manny, you put up these horses. Chico, help us get these
men inside the house. Alonzo, lend me a hand."

She stooped to help pick up the fallen soldier with corporal chevrons on his sleeve. Ben had already pulled the man
up to a sitting position. The soldier was out cold.

John heard the sheepmen talking among themselves. He
made out the words *soldados* and *ejército*. He also heard
them use the word for horses, *caballos*, as they began to help
Gale and the soldiers.

"Lieutenant, what happened?" John said to Bellaugh.

The lieutenant sagged in his arms and he lifted him, sling-
ing the man over one shoulder. Bellaugh was out cold, too,
and he was dripping blood from his right arm or shoulder.

John staggered back into the house, dripping water into
forming puddles. Bellaugh was not a large man, but he was

soaking wet and deadweight. He carried the soldier to the divan and propped him up in one corner. He sat beside him and lifted one of Bellaugh's eyelids. The man's eyes were bloodshot, probably from the stinging rain. He was unconscious, still, and a hole in his shoulder was pumping out blood. He examined the wound as Ben and Gale brought in the corporal. They laid him on the floor in front of the fire. All three were sopping wet.

"This'uns in bad shape," Ben said, his voice growly in his throat.

"I'll get a kettle of water," Gale said and sopped on wet shoes toward the kitchen.

Ben walked over to the door and closed and bolted it against the howling wind and the hurtling rain. Lightning etched zigzag patterns of liquid mercury in the black clouds and thunder rumbled in tympanic crescendos of orchestral magnitude across the skies, sounding like cannon fire inside a deep cavern.

"Lieutenant Bellaugh," John said, patting the unconscious man's cheeks. "Wake up, soldier."

Ben walked over and stood over John and the wounded Bellaugh.

"Ain't got no color in his cheeks," Ben said. "He looks done for."

"No, he's got more than a spark in him, Ben. Give me your bandanna."

Ben untied the bandanna around his neck, handed it to John. John opened the officer's shirt and saw a blue-black hole in the muscle of the shoulder. He had a few inches of flesh above the wound and he wrapped the kerchief around his arm at that spot, tying it tight. The blood stopped pumping.

"Give me a small piece of kindling, Ben," John said.

Ben rummaged through the kindling, got the smallest stick of wood he could find, and took it over to John. John slid it inside the knot, tightened the knot, then twisted the stick until the makeshift tourniquet was tight.

"I'll keep it that way until we get some clotting," John said, "then loosen it and see if he bleeds any more. We can keep tightening it until the bleeding stops or we get a regular bandage on it."

"Sounds right to me," Ben said.

Gale entered the front room lugging an iron pot sloshing with water. Ben helped her. They hung it inside the fireplace on an iron hook that dangled down from an iron plate sunk into the brick.

"I'll get some towels and bandages," she said. "That water ought to heat pretty quick. Ben, put some more wood on the fire, will you?"

"Sure," Ben said as he watched Gale scurry away, her feet making sloshing sounds as water squirted from her boots.

Ben added more cordwood to the fire, then knelt over the wounded corporal, who was still unconscious. He leaned over, cocked his head, and listened at the young man's mouth for sounds of breathing. The man was still alive, but his breath was shallow. There was blood on his shirt and both legs and Ben saw a hole high on his right chest and holes in both legs. He drew his knife and cut away his shirt and slit his trouser legs, exposing the wounds.

He felt in back of one leg to see if the bullet had gone clear through. The soldier winced when Ben touched a lumpy spot. The bullet was still in that leg, nestled just below the skin. He did the same to the other leg and couldn't find an exit wound. Nor could he detect where the bullet had wound up. Then he turned his attention to the wound in the corporal's chest. He turned him over as gently as he could and felt under the wet shirt with delicate fingers. His hand came away bloody, so he thought there must be an exit wound. He continued to feel the man's back, and just under the shoulder blade he felt a jagged hole about the size of a two-bit piece. He sighed and eased the man back down. He knew the man had lost quite a bit of blood and he also knew he had to get those lead bullets out of him or he didn't stand a Chinaman's chance in Hell to come out of this alive.

Gale returned with towels and bandages as John was cutting away the lieutenant's shirt, slitting both sleeves and

sawing off the buttons. He was using the knife he had taken
from Coyote. It was sharp and fit his hand well.

Lieutenant Bellaugh groaned and his eyelids fluttered for
a minute, but did not open. John reached behind him and
picked up his whiskey glass. There was still a swallow left in
it. He put the rim of the glass to the soldier's lips and tilted
the glass. Whiskey trickled onto the man's lips and into his
mouth. The fumes wafted to his nostrils. He gagged and
opened his eyes. John took the glass away, but held it in his
hand.

"You've lost some blood, Bellaugh," John said, "but
you're sound, I think."

Gale bent down to help Ben tend to the corporal's
wounds. She glanced at John and Bellaugh for a second and
the trace of a smile played on her lips.

"Yeah," Bellaugh said as if testing his voice. "Yeah, very
weak, Savage."

"More whiskey?"

"No. Let me clear my head. So much happened."

"You and the corporal all that's left of your troop?"

"Yeah." A faraway look came into Bellaugh's eyes. A
smoky glaze that turned wet.

John waited for Bellaugh to collect his thoughts.

"All dead. Every man jack of 'em, Savage. All dead.
God."

"Take your time, Bellaugh. Don't wear yourself out."

"You—we—you got to . . ."

"What?" John asked, when the lieutenant's voice trailed
off.

Bellaugh closed his eyes and a ripple of pain coursed
through his body. It was just a slight tremor, but John stiffened. It did not look good for Bellaugh. He had no way of
knowing how much blood the man had lost, but his face was
almost bone-white and he looked frail in his sodden uniform.

"Go on, if you can, Lieutenant. I'm listening." He put the
tumbler to Bellaugh's lips again, poured a little whiskey
through his lips. This time Bellaugh didn't choke, but smacked

his lips. He opened his eyes and stared at John as if seeing him for the first time.

"Savage?"

"Yes. I'm here. What happened."

"They come out of nowhere. Jumped us. Navajos rose up out of dirt and cactus and riders came around the little hill. Shot us to pieces. We formed a skirmish line, tried to retreat. But they were all around us, screaming and shooting. My men dropped like flies. God, it was bad."

"All Navajos?"

"No. Navajos on foot, white men on horses. We didn't have a chance. One man, the leader, he took his pistol to my wounded and executed them. He shot every man in the head. Like he enjoyed it."

"You know who it was?"

"I heard his name," Bellaugh said. "It wasn't Harley or Arlie, like I thought."

"No," John said. "It was Ollie, wasn't it?"

"How'd you know? It was Ollie. I heard it plain. That bastard."

Another tremor rippled through Bellaugh's body like static electricity. He shivered and his eyes went cloudy for a moment.

Thunder boomed outside and lightning splashed the windows with a shiny pewter sheen.

"How'd you get away?" John asked.

"Rode right through the Navajos on the ground. Dropped a couple, kept on going. Found a canyon, lost my pursuers. Corporal Dunhill and I saw the lights here and rode as fast as we could."

"Anybody follow you?"

"Didn't see anybody," Bellaugh said.

"John, the corporal's full of bullets," Ben said. "We got to dig 'em out."

Bellaugh and John looked over at the soldier lying on the floor.

"He fought bravely," Bellaugh said.

"I'm going to take a look at him, Lieutenant," John said. "You sit tight."

The water in the kettle was boiling. Steam jetted out from the fireplace and rose up the chimney with the wood smoke. Wind-driven rain battered the house and lightning generated loud thunder that rumbled like giant combers loosed from a savage sea that rolled empty barrels down the long corridor of night.

John looked at the places where Ben pointed and saw deadly wounds.

"Think you can get those bullets out, John?" Ben asked.

"I'll try. Gale, get me that bottle of whiskey to pour over my hands. I'll probe with my fingers."

Gale got up and went for the whiskey bottle.

"Might have to cut out the one that's just under the skin, Ben. Take my knife out of my belt and put it in the fire."

Ben did as he was told.

Gale poured whiskey over John's bloody hands and he started probing for one of the bullets.

Gale looked away for a minute, took a deep breath, and then watched what John was doing. The corporal showed no signs that he was feeling the pain, but he was still breathing.

Twenty minutes later, John had cut one bullet out, worked the other two free. His hands were drenched in blood and he was gripped with a great weariness as he rocked back on his haunches, sweat slick across his forehead.

"Got any balm or unguent, Gale?" John asked.

"I do," she said.

"Pack those wounds with whatever you have and put a pillow under the corporal's head. He's breaking out in a fever. I doubt if he will last until morning with that much blood lost."

"Savage," Bellaugh said, his voice weaker than before.

"Yes, Lieutenant?"

"If we don't make it, will you tell Sheriff Wilts in Tucson what happened? He'll get word to the fort."

"You'll make it, Bellaugh. Clive."

Clive tried to laugh but the pain cut off his breath.

"Promise me you'll tell Wilts about Ollie and a man named Crudder."

"I will. The man who executed your men is named Oliver Hobart. I've been hunting him a long time. Ever since he murdered my family in Colorado."

A light came into Bellaugh's eyes. He stared hard at John.

"John Savage. You're that Savage?"

"I am."

"Lord," Bellaugh breathed. "And this Ollie is . . ."

"The man I'm hunting, Clive. When I find him, I'm going to nail him to the barn door and set the barn on fire. He's got a lot to answer for."

"You get him, Savage," Bellaugh said. "You get him for me."

"I'll get him for both of us, Lieutenant."

"And for my men."

"For all the people he murdered, Clive. I'll get him."

John paused, then stood up, his hand red in the lamplight.

"That's a promise, sir," he said.

And Lieutenant Bellaugh managed a smile.

22

THE STRONG WINDS LINGERED AWHILE AFTER THE STORM HAD
passed, shortly before midnight. Ben stayed with the wounded
corporal, while Gale slept. John laid Bellaugh on his back
atop the divan so he could catch some shut-eye. He dozed in a
chair, listening to the rain diminish, the thunder fade away in
the distance.

Corporal Dunhill had stopped bleeding, but he had lost so
much blood, he weakened and died shortly before dawn.
Ben woke John to tell him.

"You go on out to the bunkhouse, Johnny. I'll stay with
the lieutenant." Ben had gotten some sleep, but he was still
tired.

"I don't know if Bellaugh's going to make it," John said.

"Nothin' you can do. Get some sleep, Johnny."

Shortly after dawn, John awoke. The sheepherders were
already up and making coffee, cooking breakfast. He told
them about the corporal's death and expected the lieutenant
would die, too.

"We will let the sheep out when the sun has dried the
grass," one of them said. "If you need help, we will come."

John went into the house to find Ben sound asleep. Bellaugh

was asleep, too, his breathing thready. His face was still pale, but he had no fever. Whether or not that was a good sign, John did not know. Gale was in the kitchen, trying to be quiet. He whispered to her about the corporal.

"I know," she whispered back. "We'll put him in a wagon, take him to Tucson sometime today."

"You might have two in that wagon," John said, still whispering.

She nodded.

"I checked his pulse," she said. "It was very weak."

"Did you check Ben's?"

Gale gave out an almost-silent laugh.

"I should have," she said. "He's dead to the world, poor man."

"We'll be up at the mine, if you need us," John said.

"I'll pack you a lunch, give you some vittles. You can cook up there. There are plates and utensils in one of the cabinets."

"We'll be fine," he said. "Thanks."

As John made preparations to leave, he saddled both his and Ben's horses. He would let Ben sleep as long as possible. They had much to do. He was worried about Bellaugh and dreaded going back into the house to check on him. Yet he had sensed the night before that Clive knew he was going to die. His last words about getting Hobart let him know that the lieutenant never expected to ride out after the murderous outlaw.

It was sad, he thought. Bellaugh was a young man in his prime. He probably had a good future in the army. He had been cut down mercilessly by a man who didn't deserve to breathe the same air as Bellaugh.

Ben was still sound asleep when John returned to the house.

Gale met him in the front room, holding a flour sack.

"I'll put this next to the ore sample," she said. "Are you ready to leave? It's still early."

She looked so grandmotherly that John felt a tug at his

heart. She had such a radiant face at that moment, he was deeply touched. He felt a sadness at leaving her alone in the house with one dead man, another probably dying. She had lit a single lamp and its orange glow softened one side of her face so that she looked almost youthful.

Outside, the dawn was just hovering below the horizon, wiping out all but the morning star from the bluing sky. Birds chirped and a mist rose from the grasses on a field surrounded by low mountains in solemn shadow.

"Yes, as soon as I can rouse old Ben there," he said.

"Oh, he's not so old," she said, and there was a coyness to her tone that he found charming.

"No, I reckon not," he said. "How's Lieutenant Bellaugh doing?"

"His breathing is very shallow. And I could hear a slight rattling in his throat when I bent over him a while ago."

"I hope he pulls through, Gale."

"So do I," she said, and her breathy whisper sounded like a prayer.

John stood next to Ben, shook his shoulder gently.

"Ben," he said. "Time to get up."

Ben's eyes fluttered open and he jerked up to a sitting position. He drew his legs up and massaged both knees. He rubbed grains of sleep from his eyes and looked at Gale.

"You look like an angel," he said.

Gale's face turned pink with a sudden blush.

She made a slight curtsy to acknowledge the compliment.

Then she turned and set the sack of foodstuffs down on the table next to the chunk of ore and scurried off to the kitchen. Ben got up and stretched. A moment later, Gale returned with two cups of steaming coffee. She made both men sit down before she handed them their cups.

"Still wet outside?" Ben asked, blowing steam off his coffee.

"Pretty wet," John said. The coffee warmed him, cleared the night phlegm from his throat.

"There's coffee in the bag," Gale said, "and a pot in one

of those cupboards in the lab. Clarence liked his Arbuckle's. I'm sending you two pounds, and we'll come by with more in a week, if you're still there."

"We shouldn't be more than a week or so, if my plan works," John said.

"That's pretty fast," Ben said, swishing the coffee around his mouth to cool it some. "Hobart's probably in Mexico by now."

John said nothing. He knew that Hobart had ways of finding out things that mattered to him. Very few people had known about the diggings in Colorado, yet Hobart knew just where to come and how many men he would need to slaughter everyone there. He had a hunch that Ollie knew people in Tucson who would give him the information he wanted, for a price. Gold made men mad. It also made them greedy and willing to sacrifice honesty and honor for a taste of it.

Ben and John said their good-byes and left Gale with Lieutenant Bellaugh, who was still alive despite great odds.

By mid-afternoon they were on the mesa and had set their bedrolls, saddlebags, and rifles inside the lab building. John found all the pots and pans, plates, and eating utensils, and there was plenty of wood to cook and keep them warm at night.

"I wonder what happened to that Injun you caught, John. Coyote. Think he was part of that bunch that jumped the soldiers?"

"Probably. I wouldn't worry about him. We're leaving first thing in the morning for Tucson."

"You're just goin' to ride in there, pretty as you please, and pay no nevermind that Hobart's bunch might be there?"

"Yep, I am. Goin' straight to the assay office with that chunk of ore and some of those pouches of dust."

"You have to show the assayer the gold dust?"

"I want to make his eyes wide," John said.

"If I didn't know you better, Johnny, I'd say you'd gone plumb loco."

"Maybe. I have a hunch the word will get out pretty quick

once that assayer sees what we have. And I'm counting on his having a big mouth."

"You goin' to see that Sheriff Wilts that the lieutenant told you about?"

"Yes, but I'm sure Gale will beat us to it."

"She goin' up there today?"

"If Bellaugh can make the trip," John said.

At dawn the next morning, John and Ben were already riding toward Tucson, carrying the chunk of rich ore and several bags of gold dust they still had from the diggings in Colorado.

Gold, John thought, was like a magnet. It drew people to it, cast them under its magic spell.

He hoped Hobart would be the first to succumb to its golden allure.

23

THE SIGN ON THE ADOBE STORE WINDOW READ: HIRAM L. ABERNATHY, PROP. ASSAYS, MINING CLAIMS, NOTARY PUBLIC. The morning sun was the only light on the street and halfway down, the small building was still in shadow. John could see a man moving around inside the store brandishing a feather duster. Motes of dust danced in his wake like mothlings stirred from their night beds.

Ben and John tied their horses to hitchrings embedded in an adobe cairn in front of the boardwalk, and walked inside. Ben carried a gunny sack with the ore sample, John had his saddlebags slung over his shoulder, one pouch bulging with sacks of gold dust.

Abernathy looked up at the big clock on his wall as the two men entered his store. A bell tinkled above it, bobbing on a slender bar of metal. The sound startled Ben and he staggered to the side in a misstep. Abernathy chuckled.

"That's just my warning bell," the man said, "so's I can hear if anybody comes in while I'm in the back room working at my trade."

"You the assayer?" John asked.

"Hiram Abernathy at your service, sir. What can I do for

you on this fine morning? Early as it is, we're open for business."

"You get much business?" Ben asked, hefting the heavy burlap sack.

"Not so much, not so steady, but tollible, sir, tollible. What you got in your sack?"

"Gold ore," John said, his voice booming in the small room. "From the old Gill mine."

"Knowed old Clarence," Abernathy said. "He was good people. Gale sell his mine to you boys?"

"Yes," John said. "We have some ore we took out yesterday. Got more of it up there and we got some dust we want weighed."

"You boys must have been workin' hard. Where'd you get the dust?"

"We have a place," John said.

"Not up on that shelf."

"You ask a lot of questions, Mr. Abernathy," John said. "We want an assay and a weighing, that's all."

"Sure, sure, glad to do it. Let me see your ore, then we can weigh your dust."

Ben thought Abernathy's eyes would pop out of his skull when he slid the ore from the sack. The assayer turned the ore over and over in his hands and his eyes bulged even more.

"Take me a day or so to get you an assay on this. I'll have you sign some papers, which I will also sign, and then we'll both be protected."

"Fine," John said.

Abernathy took the ore into a back room. Ben and John could hear him load it onto a shelf. When he returned, he was smiling. He brought with him a legal document and a receipt. He wrote down all the pertinent information.

"Now, your name, sir, if you please?"

"John Savage."

Abernathy wrote down the name. John watched him closely, saw no sign that his name registered with the man. The assayer signed all the papers and wrote out a receipt for the ore sample. He gave John a copy that matched his own. He slid his copy under the counter, out of sight. John folded his receipt and handed it to Ben, who tucked it inside his shirt.

"Now let's take a look at your dust. Gold is at sixteen dollars the ounce."

John reached into his saddlebag and set six sacks of gold dust on the counter. Abernathy's eyes strained to get out of their sockets. These were large leather pouches and when he lifted one, his mouth twisted into a half smile and his nose wrinkled.

"My, you two have been busy," he said.

Abernathy opened one pouch and looked inside, eyes wide as a bird egg.

He set the scales.

"I should pour this out," he said. "Sack weighs so much."

"Do what you have to do," John said.

"Well, let's see here," Abernathy said. He poured the gold dust into a small funneled container on the scale. He reached under the counter, pulled out a piece of paper and the stub of a lead pencil.

He marked the weight of the dust and wrote it down on the piece of paper. He hummed to himself while he did this.

"Now I'll just weigh this pouch empty, and we might be able to speed up the process. Looks like each sack weighs about the same. Unless you want a real accurate figure on how much your dust weighs."

"Close is good enough," John said. "We're in something of a hurry."

"We'll do it that way, then. You want to cash any of this dust in for greenbacks?"

"No."

Abernathy removed the container with the dust and weighed the leather pouch. He wrote down that figure.

"Now," he said, "we'll just weigh these other pouches and see how many ounces in each, subtracting the weight of the pouch."

Ben watched Abernathy, who hummed some tuneless ditty while he weighed and subtracted and wrote down figures on the piece of paper. When he was finished, he handed the sacks to John, one in each hand. John put them back in his saddle-bag.

"My, my," Abernathy said to himself as he totaled the fig-ures. "You have a goodly amount of dust here. Is this all you have?"

"No," John said. "We just brought those in because they were handy."

Ben's eyes went wide, but he kept his thoughts to himself. He poked his tongue into one cheek, pooching it out as though he had a lollypop in it.

Abernathy turned the piece of paper around, pushed it to-ward John.

"Those are the ounces, and I took the liberty of multiply-ing those by sixteen to give you a dollar figure on what your dust is worth at this moment."

John studied the figures, but did not pick up the piece of paper.

"Sounds right," he said.

He left the paper on the counter and Abernathy made no more mention of it. Instead, he licked his lips, looking like the cat who swallowed the goldfish out of the bowl, his eyes protruding like a pair of marbles in a bowl of mush.

"See you in a couple of days," John said. "Thank you, Mr. Abernathy."

"Yes, you come back, sir. I'll have your assay ready for you."

"At first glance, Mr. Abernathy, does the ore look promis-ing to you?" John asked.

Abernathy cleared his throat.

"Well, hard to say. Have to do some checking, some weighing. And, as you may know, an assay can only assess what's measurable. If you have a vein, it could peter out after a couple of inches, or it could go several feet, high or low, deep or shallow."

"I understand," John said.

"Ah, do you have any more like that one?" Abernathy asked. "None of my business, of course, but just curious."

John thought a moment as he looked into Abernathy's eyes. They were lit up like a pair of glowworms.

He looked at Ben and winked with the eye that Abernathy could not see.

"I got a couple of wheelbarrows full of ore just like that chunk I brought in."

Abernathy swallowed, which seemed to act on his eyes, both of which widened and swelled like a pair of roasting marshmallows on a stick.

"Well, now," Abernathy clucked without making a sentence or expressing his thought.

"See you in a couple of days, Mr. Abernathy," John said again, holding back his smile. He and Ben walked out of the building and onto the street. They untied their horses and rode off at a slow pace.

"Where now?" Ben asked.

"First to see Sheriff Wilts," John said.

"Then back to the mine?"

"No," John said, "I want to take a look at that saloon Crudder mentioned when we were in the canyon."

"Hobart's hangout?"

"That's the place," John said.

"Johnny, you're playin' with fire, ain't you?"

John thought about Abernathy and his reaction not only to the ore sample but to the sacks of gold dust. He had seen such looks before, in Cherry Creek, Denver, Cheyenne. Gold did funny things to a man, any man, and Abernathy's excitement was plain to see. If his hunch was right, the man would brag about his morning's business to anyone who would listen. And there probably wasn't a man in Tucson who wouldn't.

"Playing with fire, Ben?" John said. "I sure hope so."

24

VENDORS BEGAN TO SET OUT THEIR WARES AS THE SUN ROSE higher, splashing light on the adobe buildings. Unmarked and painted pottery sat on wooden boards nailed into square platforms. Women draped serapes and rugs over sawhorses and displayed turquoise trinkets, bracelets, necklaces, rings, spoons, knives, and forks, attached to cloth-covered boards leaned against the front of buildings. Mexicans drove *carretas*, small carts, drawn by burros, down every street, hawking their wares of copper pots, fresh chickens, eggs, piglets in wooden cages, pitchers and bowls, wooden toys painted with ancient Navajo symbols.

Log roof beams jutted from the top floors of adobe buildings and they read signs on false fronts that proclaimed ABARROTES, COMIDAS, and TORTILLERILLA. Indian men and women, Hopis, wore plum-colored shirts and sat in shady spots hawking beads and deerskin moccasins, purses and belt pouches, knives made from wagon springs lying next to beaded sheaths.

The air smelled clean and fresh, and the smells of corn and flour tortillas wafted on the morning air. The carts stirred up little dust in the damp streets and the scent of wood smoke was pleasant, mixed with the smoke of strong tobacco and charcoal. Two large wagons loomed ahead of Ben and John, lumbering down the street with flocks of boys on either side chattering in Spanish.

The wagons were stacked high with pine coffins, whip-sawed boards nailed together with square nails from the local foundry. The mules left signs of their passing in steaming clumps on the street, and that smell mingled with the taint of urine emptied from full bladders.

"Are them coffins?" Ben asked as if he already knew the question was inane.

"What do you think?" John said.

"They sure is a passel of 'em."

"I counted twelve. Six in each wagon."

"Where they takin' them?"

"Let's find out," John said.

They followed the wagons for another two blocks. The lead wagon stopped in front of a false front erected on an adobe building. The driver set the brake, climbed down and walked around it, then stepped up on the boardwalk. The sign in the window read: PERCIVAL MARLEY & SON, UNDERTAKERS.

A man came out of the establishment and spoke to the driver, pointed to the end of the block, and made a circling motion with his hands. Ben and John rode up close enough to hear him.

"Take them around to the alley in back. There's a loading dock where you can set 'em."

"You got somebody to help us, Mr. Marley?"

"My son will be waitin' for you. Get along now. You're blockin' the street."

The driver touched a finger to the brim of his derby hat and walked back around the wagon.

"We're goin' out back, Jenks. Just foller me."

Jenks nodded. He was a younger man, no more than fifteen or sixteen, John figured, and he was hatless. Both men wore suspenders and heavy work boots. They smelled of pine shavings and wagon grease. The mules slapped their tails at flies and shook their heads to get rid of the pests.

The wagons pulled away as Marley went back inside. He was a florid-faced man, dressed in a black suit. He wore a black string tie that made him look even more slender than he was. Ben and John could hear him yelling to someone in the back of the large, oblong room that was filled with open caskets on display.

"Looks like that gent's got him some business," Ben said.

"I wonder," John said, "if his customers are wearing U.S. Army uniforms."

"Hey, I never thought of that," Ben said. "D'you suppose . . ."

"I do," John said and clucked to his horse, prodding his flanks with his spurs. They rode another block and stopped in front of a small building, also adobe, with a false front. The lettering on the window announced that it was the sheriff's office, and beneath it, the name SAM WILTS, SHERIFF.

There was a hitchrail out front. A half dozen saddled horses were lined up, their reins wrapped around the top rail. Next to the horses there was a small burro, a blanket for a saddle, wearing a rope bridle, tied to a post.

Both John and Ben noticed the A brands on the hips of the horses.

"Looks like army," Ben said.

"And no soldiers anywhere in sight."

"What're you getting' at, John?"

"Maybe nothing." John's eyes narrowed in thought, but he didn't elaborate. All of the rifle scabbards were empty, and there was a long rope through all the bit rings.

The two men tied their horses to vacant posts and walked into the sheriff's office. A man wearing a badge sat behind a small cherrywood desk, his protruding belly pouring over his gunbelt. He had a handlebar moustache and flaring sideburns that fuzzed out gray at the ends. His small wet mouth was tobacco-stained a mottled brown, and his small receding chin was almost lost in the bulge of his thick neck. A lean slat of a man stood to one side, arms folded, a deputy's badge on his vest, while a small Mexican man, holding a straw sombrero in his hand, stood in front of the desk, his black hair sodden with sweat, glistening like black velvet in the sunlight that blared from the front window.

Sheriff Sam Wilts looked at John and Ben, his eyebrows arching in a silent inquisitive signal.

"Gentleman," Wilts said in a noncommittal tone.

"You Sheriff Wilts?" John said.

"That depends. He owe you money?"

Ben snickered.

The deputy chortled.

The Mexican's eyes glittered under hooded cowls.

"If you are Wilts," John said, "I have a message for you from Lieutenant Clive Bellaugh."

John spoke so soft the sheriff and deputy both had to lean forward to hear from him. But now he had their complete attention.

"You what?"

"You heard me," John said, his patience thinning down to the size of a wheat straw.

"Bellaugh?"

"That's the one," John said.

"What's the message?"

John told him about the detachment being jumped by some white men and Navajos. He told Wilts that only Bellaugh and Dunhill had escaped.

"Both were badly wounded when they rode up to the Gill ranch. Corporal Dunhill died, and Bellaugh might be dead by now. He was shot up pretty bad. Lost a lot of blood."

"The hell you say."

"The message from Bellaugh to you is this, Sheriff. He knows the name of two men who attacked him."

"He does?"

"That's what I said."

"What are the names?"

John let several seconds pass by. He wanted both Wilts and his deputy to keep that curious expression on their faces. He wanted to see how those expressions changed when he mentioned the names of the two men.

"Crudder and Hobart," John said.

The deputy's mouth dropped open like the trapdoor on a gallows stage.

Sheriff Wilts pooched out his lips as his eyes bulged like a pair of bubbles in a pot of boiling grits.

He scooted back in his chair and looked hard at the Mexican.

"Manolito," he said, "do you know those men?"

Manolito shook his head.

"I do not know them, but I heard their names called when they were fighting the soldiers."

"Manolito here was hunting rattlesnakes when he heard the soldiers coming. Then he heard the ambush. He brought those horses back. And he brought the dead men here in a wagon last night. He said the outlaws and the Indians killed all the soldiers. He didn't know that two got away. The others were run off or captured by Indians."

"Did he say where Hobart and Crudder went?" John asked.

"He said they rode south, toward Mexico."

"Do you know Hobart and Crudder, Sheriff?"

"I know of them. They stayed in Tucson a while back, then up and disappeared. I figured good riddance."

"Didn't you know Hobart was a wanted man?"

"I do now. I found a flyer in my stack of wanted dodgers. Why? You know this jasper?"

"No, I don't know him," John said.

"Who are you anyway? I don't believe I caught your names?"

"I'm John Savage. This is Ben Russell."

"You wanted for anything?"

"I don't think so," John said.

"How come you're in Tucson and bringin' me that message from Lieutenant Bellaugh?"

"We bought the Gill mine from Gale. I brought in an ore sample this morning. Bellaugh knew we were headed for Tucson."

Wilts opened a drawer in his desk and picked up a stack of wanted flyers. He riffled through them while the deputy looked on. When he was finished, he put the flyers back in his drawer and closed it.

"No dodgers on you two," Wilts said.

"I'm glad we're not under suspicion for delivering a message," John said, his words laden with sarcasm.

"Yeah," Ben said, "we're just citizens doin' our duty."

Wilts glared at Ben.

"I thank you, gents," Wilts said. "Anything else?"

"Not as far as we're concerned," John said. "We'll be heading out."

"See you again, maybe."

"Aren't you goin' after Hobart?" Ben asked. "Formin' a posse or somethin'?"

"No," Wilts said. "He's out of my jurisdiction. Probably settin' in Nogales, nigh on a hunnert miles from here. If he's in Mexico, I couldn't go after him anyway. I'll let the army know, and they'll tell the U.S. marshal, maybe."

"Do you know why that detachment was hunting Hobart?" John asked. It was not a friendly question.

"Well, there was a mine robbed, and the army said they'd handle it."

"Just what do you do here, Sheriff? Let the army capture your outlaws?"

"Mister, you just stepped over the line. I do my job, that's all you need to know."

John touched a finger to the brim of his hat and smiled.

"See you, Sheriff."

"Sam," the deputy said, "you never heard that man's name before?"

"What man's name, Leon?"

"That man there, the young 'un."

"Nope. Why?"

"John Savage, ain't it?" Leon said.

"That's right," John said.

"Wasn't you the one out in Coloraddy what was robbed, your family kilt and all. And wasn't Hobart the man who done it?"

"You've got a very bright deputy, Sheriff," John said.

Then he and Ben walked out the door, leaving the three men inside wearing blank masks that might have been sculpted out of wet putty.

After John and Ben saddled up and rode away, Ben blurted out what was on his mind.

"Mexico," he said. "We goin' after Hobart? Couldn't be hard to find him if he's just over the border."

"No, Ben," we're not going to chase Ollie anymore. He's going to come to us."

"What makes you think he'll come back to Tucson?"

"It only takes one," John said.

"One what?"

"One greedy man. And we have one right here in Tucson, I'm pretty sure."

"We do? Who?"

"That assayer. Abernathy. I'll bet he knows where Hobart is and has already sent word down to him about you and me and our rock of gold."

"John, you just surprise the hell out of me ever' time I think I got you figgered out. What makes you think Abernathy knows where Hobart is and is going to send word to him?"

"That other mine," John said. "Somebody had to tell Ollie about the gold. And who knew? Abernathy."

"Well, I'll be damned. That sure could be, Johnny. It sure could."

"I'd bet on it," John said.

John studied the various buildings as they rode through town. "There it is," he said when they reached the edge of town.

"There's what?" Ben said.

"The La Copa. The cantina where Hobart hangs out."

"We going inside?"

"No, not now," John said as they rode on by.

Just south of town, they saw the tracks of a shod horse heading south. They were visible in the once-damp earth that was now drying fast and deep under the radiance of the blazing sun. Fresh horse tracks heading south into a desolate land where nobody on a good horse had any legitimate reason to go.

And Nogales, Mexico, was less than a week's ride from Tucson.

25

BEN WAS TERRIFIED OF SCORPIONS.

John had found that out shortly after he and Ben had begun melting down the gold dust in iron ladles, streaming the liquid into porous volcanic rock that they placed in the mine. In the heat of the afternoon, Ben had seen something at the edge of the mineshaft, something that looked like a broken twig. He had reached down to pick it up when the creature struck at him, jabbing his fingertip with the barb on the end of its tail.

Ben screamed and doubled over in pain. The scorpion stalked Ben, its tail curled up for another strike.

"Get it, Johnny, get it quick."

Ben stood there, frozen in terror, holding his injured finger which had begun to swell. The scorpion struck at Ben's boot and the blood drained from his face. He fell over in a dead swoon.

John squashed the scorpion with his boot, then knelt beside Ben. He lifted his friend off the dirt and gently tapped both cheeks to revive him.

Ben moaned in pain as his eyes widened in fear.

"I got him," John said. "The scorpion's dead."

"Where is it?"

"Right over there." John pointed to the dead hulk. Ben scooted away from it. He gibbered to himself the rest of the day, and that night he shook out his bedroll and swept the floor of the lab to make sure no scorpions were hiding inside.

"I didn't know you were scared of scorpions, Ben," John said the next morning.

"Well, I sure as hell am, the little buggers."

"Think you can hold the fort while I ride into Tucson?"

"What for?"

"I'm going to pick up the ore and get our assay from Abernathy."

"And leave me here by myself?"

"No need for both of us to go in. Besides, Gale might come by any day now."

Ben eyed John with suspicion. He glared at the ground for yards around, looking for any sign of movement.

"Well?" John said.

"I reckon. You go on."

"You keep rubbing that salve on your finger. I don't think you got stung badly."

Ben screwed up his face like a man about to cry.

"Bad enough," he grumped.

"See you tonight," John said, and climbed into the saddle. "Keep your eyes peeled for Gale."

"I'm keepin' 'em peeled for scorpions and rattlers," Ben said and walked back into the coolness of the lab.

———————

ABERNATHY BROUGHT OUT THE ORE SAMPLE, ALONG WITH A FLOUR sack, and laid them on the counter.

"Got your report," he said, his fingers fidgety on the counter. He kept looking over John's shoulder as if he were expecting someone to walk in at any moment. "That'll be thirty dollars, sir."

"Let me see the report."

"Surely. I have it right here." Abernathy leaned down and pulled a sheet of paper from a shelf beneath the counter.

John looked at it.

"Are these figures correct, Mr. Abernathy?"

"I don't make mistakes. That ore sample reckons at eight hundred dollars the ton. Mighty rich."

John paid him the thirty dollars in greenbacks.

"I brought you a sack since you're on horseback. 'Stead of a box."

"I appreciate that."

Abernathy slid the rock into the sack, lifted it, and handed it to John.

"You got any more samples you want assayed, you bring 'em in."

"I will," John said. "I assume the results of your assay are confidential."

Abernathy huffed up, expanding his chest like a pouter pigeon.

"Of course," he said with an air of indignation. "We observe the highest propriety in these matters."

"I'm sure you do," John said and touched fingers to the brim of his hat in a farewell salute.

Abernathy had broken out in a sweat when he handed the sack over to John. It glistened on his forehead like a patina of machine oil. The man was nervous as hell, John thought, and he was sure he knew why. He had no doubt that Abernathy was a Judas who had betrayed him to Oliver Hobart. He smiled.

"I should have given him a tip for that," he said to himself as he packed away the ore in his saddlebags.

26

NOT LONG AFTER JOHN HAD RIDDEN OFF TO TUCSON, BEN HEARD the rumble of a wagon down on the flat. He felt a surge of blood through his veins. He grabbed his rifle, which was leaning against the wall by the front door, and stepped outside into the sunlight.

He crept up to the edge of the tabletop and peered down into the valley. Dust spooled out from behind the wheels of a wagon drawn by a pair of horses. Another horse was tied to the end of the wagon. And the wagon was flanked by six men on horseback. Two people sat on the seat, one driving, the other holding a rifle that glinted in the sun.

Ben stood up and waved.

Gale, who was driving the wagon, waved back. When she came to the road, she turned the team and headed up the slope where Ben was waiting.

She drove the wagon up on the flat, next to the laboratory, and turned it around to face the way back down the road. Ben walked over and saw the sadness on Gale's face. He hooked a thumb over her shoulder and he walked to the side of the wagon and looked inside. There were two bodies in the bed, each wrapped in a gray blanket. When he walked back to help Gale down, there were tears on her face and her eyes were cloudy with mist.

"The lieutenant died," he said.

"Last night, Ben."

She set the brake and took Ben's hand, then stepped down off the wagon.

"You get down, too, Romero," she said to the sheepherder who had been on the seat with her.

Romero climbed down the other side. The mounted riders, all sheepherders, lined up along the edge of the mesa, their rifles pointed straight up at the sky as they watched the valley.

"You came with guards?" Ben said. She did not take her hand out of his.

"They will stay with you while Romero drives the wagon to Tucson. I've given him a note to give Sheriff Wilts."

"You're staying here?" he said.

"Let's go inside. It's too hot to stay out here. Come on, Romero. Will you please carry in those bags of foodstuffs?"

Romero, a stocky man in his forties, with strong hands and flinty black eyes, coal-black hair, high cheekbones, and a wide square jaw, nodded and walked around to the back of the wagon.

Ben and Gale entered the lab where the air was cool.

He noticed that she was wearing a pistol, and her gunbelt was full of .44-caliber ammunition.

When Romero walked in a few minutes later, he carried a large sack of airtights and other foodstuffs. He walked to the back and put the goods on the counter.

"You can untie my horse and tie him up outside," she said. "Then you'd better get into town. You be sure and give Sheriff Wilts my letter."

"I will do this, señora," he said. "Do not worry. I will come back tonight."

"Good-bye, Romero. *Ten cuidado.* Be careful," she said and closed the door after he left the lab.

Ben heard the wagon rumble off, leaving a great silence in its wake. He looked at Gale, who seemed ready to sag to the floor.

"You're tired," he said.

"Yes. Let's sit down for a few minutes, Ben. Maybe I'll make us some tea. I found some in my cupboard and thought to bring it. It's real tea, from China."

"I never got a taste for it," he said, leading her to the back of the lab. There, she saw that Ben and John had set two chairs on opposite sides of a table. She felt a tug at her heart, as if an unseen hand had pulled one of her arteries. Clarence had made those chairs and that table. She remembered how proud he had been every time he turned out a piece of furniture on his lathe and workbench. There were so many things inside the lab that reminded her of Clarence. Now there was an emptiness inside her as she thought of him. She sat down and sighed. Ben sat down, too, and looked over at her, a sign of concern on his face.

"You should have stayed home," he said. "It's just too hot outside for a trip like that. Not a speck of shade on the road, and maybe hostile Injuns about."

"Ben, I've been in this country so long, I don't mind the heat that much. Sometimes I think I'm part Mexican and maybe part Navajo. This land has a way of getting inside a person. When I'm working with my sheep, with the men who work for me, and knowing what I know about their backgrounds, I feel like one of them. I'm so used to speaking Spanish, I think in Spanish most of the time. I declare, someday, if I live long enough, I'll probably forget how to speak English."

Ben laughed, and then she laughed with him.

"I think I know what you mean, Gale. Johnny and I haven't been out here that long, but sometimes, of an evenin', I stand outside and look up at the sky and down at the valley and think I might have been here forever. And sometimes, I think I want to be here forever."

Gale laughed a small laugh.

"The land will get to you, if you stay long enough," she said. Then she turned serious and Ben's senses perked up. "Ben, do you have a home to go back to?"

"I guess not. Not anymore. I called Missouri home once.

Then I got used to Colorado. The mountains. But I got no home, really."

"Maybe you might think of settling here, here in Arizona."

"I never thought of it. Not in a while, anyway. Me'n Johnny have been huntin' Hobart so long, I ain't been able to think much beyond it."

"I think John's a very troubled young man," she said.

There was a pause.

"Don't you?" she asked, her voice soft.

"I think he's a-wrestlin' with some kind of demon. There's been so much killin' and I think he's gettin' plumb tired of it."

"And you?" she asked in that same soft voice.

"Yeah, I reckon." He paused. "I think it's that pistol his pa left him, one he done over and put all that silver on it. Johnny seems to think it's got some kind of curse on it."

"That's silly," she said. "A gun is just a tool, like a hammer or a hatchet."

"Not that Colt he carries. It's something bigger'n ordinary to his mind."

"Maybe because his daddy gave it to him."

"Maybe. He cottoned to his pa all right. They was real close."

Gale got up from the table and found a teakettle in the cupboard. She filled it with water and put it on the stove.

"This got any coals in it?" she said.

"Yes'm. I'll stick some kindlin' in and fire it up."

While the stove was getting hot, the two sat down. Gale reached across the table and took Ben's hands in her own.

"You've got good strong hands," she said.

"Thank you, ma'am."

"Ben, since meeting you and John, I've been thinking about you both a lot. But especially you. I'm wondering if you'd consider stayin' on my ranch when you and John are finished with this Hobart business."

"I dunno."

"Well, I don't have much to offer. But I'm a good cook

and I'd pay you good wages to help me tend my sheep.
Might even set you up on a spread of your own after a while,
if you wanted."

"It sounds mighty nice right now. I just don't know what
Johnny's gonna want to do. He might get Hobart. Hobart
might get him. I just can't see into the future."

"I understand," she said. "You don't have to make your
mind up right away. I just wanted to plant a little seed in your
mind, Ben. If something happened to me, I don't have any
kin to leave my property to. I'm just about finished writing
my book and if I can get it published, why, we might both
give up ranching and sail the seven seas."

There was a twinkle in her eye when she said that and
Ben felt a mellow warmth sweep through him. She squeezed
his hands, then released them. The teakettle whistled on the
stove and both of them jumped as if snakebit.

Gale opened a tin of orange pekoe and pekoe and
spooned the leaves into two tin cups. She poured hot water
in the cups and then placed them on the table. She sat down.

"Let the tea steep for a few minutes," she said.

"Yes'm."

Ben thought about what Gale had said to him. She was a
comely woman, and he a lonely man. But he knew nothing
about sheep and he wondered if she wanted to hire him or
marry him. She might be a hungry woman, and his instincts
told him to run from her as fast as he could move his legs
and feet. As soon as he thought this, he felt guilty. The
woman was being kind to him and he shouldn't harbor such
opinions without proof.

They drank their tea without saying anything. The vapors
rose like tiny shawls from their cups and the smell was
pleasing to both of them.

Sunlight streamed through the windows with slanted
columns of light the color of sand. Ben felt drawn to this
strong woman with her snowy hair and pretty blue eyes who
smelled of rosewater. She might be a woman to ride the river
with, he thought. More than that, she almost felt like home.
His emotions rose up in him and he had to turn away from

her, had to stop the rush of thoughts that were turning his muscles to mush, his mind to persimmon jelly.

"A penny," she said.

"Huh?"

"I'm offerin' you a penny for those thoughts of yours, Ben."

He laughed, suddenly self-conscious.

"Oh, I don't know as I could express 'em real well, Gale."

"Too bad. I was hoping you would confide in me. As if I was your friend."

"You are my friend," he said. "And I'm mighty glad to be in your company."

Despite himself, Ben blushed. His face turned a pale crimson and he flashed her an embarrassed smile.

"I'm glad to hear that," she said. "I feel the same way. I feel, Ben, as if I've known you for a good long time, longer than we've actually known each other. And I find your company very pleasant."

"You're a good woman, Gale. And life is mighty short. I—I just ain't handy with the right words."

"You don't have to say anything, Ben. Just enjoy your tea, while I enjoy you."

He felt as if he were melting inside. The way she talked, the way she looked at him. He was melting and he hadn't had such feelings in so long he had forgotten the youth that had experienced them. So many years gone by, and nothing much to show for it. How could he explain such things to anyone, much less Gale Gill?

He couldn't, he knew. Feelings were like smoke. You couldn't rope 'em, you couldn't hog-tie 'em. You just felt them. Felt them real deep inside, like the taste of good wine or the scent of a flower early in the morning.

They heard hoofbeats, then the creak of leather, the jangle of metal rings. Then pounding footsteps, a loud knock on the door.

"Come in," Gale called.

The door opened and one of the sheepherders burst through it, his eyes wide.

"There is a rider," he said. "He is coming. He is . . ."

"Slow down, Fidel," she said. "Is he coming from the north or from the south?"

"He comes from the south."

Gale's eyes flared. Ben set his tea down and scraped his chair as he climbed out of it.

"That ain't Johnny comin'," he said.

"Trouble?" Gale asked as Ben bolted for the door, brushing Fidel aside.

"It sure as hell ain't good news," he said.

Gale took Fidel by the arm and they walked back outside together.

"You be ready," she said as he climbed back on his horse.

Fidel turned his horse and galloped to the edge of the tabletop. Gale walked slowly to where Ben was standing. He was staring down at the valley, shading his eyes from the sun.

"Who is it?" she asked.

"I don't know," he said. "But it sure as hell ain't Johnny."

The rider was turning onto the road that led up to the mesa and the mine. His face was shaded by the brim of his hat. A rifle jutted from its boot, and sunlight glinted off the cartridges in his gunbelt.

He looked like a man with a purpose as he rode on, seemingly fearless, right into a half dozen guns that were aimed straight at him.

Ben's eyes narrowed to dark slits.

The rider, he thought, was either mighty bold or plumb crazy.

27

JOHN NOONED IN THE DUBIOUS SHADE OF A SMALL BUTTE several hundred yards off the road. He chewed on boiled mutton slabbed between two halves of a dried biscuit Ben had cooked the day before. Dry-throated, he sipped warm water from his wooden canteen and stared at the blue sky with small cottony clouds moving so slow they almost seemed motionless. He had seen no travelers on the road south, nor had he expected any in the heat of the day.

John gazed at a land of sunshine and shadows, so serene, so peaceful under the blue sky. He marveled at the many shapes, the ancient formations that seemed as if they had been built by gods. The land seemed barren, but oddly golden, with a subtle mixture of cinnamon, lavender, and autumnal brown, as enticing as a painted lady in an enormous room, lying on a majestic couch draped with throws and shawls. He felt the land come into him as if its immense power had the ability to enslave a man's heart, capture his soul.

A lizard slithered across a shady rock, seeking the warmth of the sun, its tiny eyes glittering like a pair of jewels, its velvety skin woven of yellow-and-blue stripes, its muscles fluid and flowing, its tail twitching like a magic wand. Flies buzzed and hunted for blood or droppings from his food, their melodies an undertone to his thoughts, minor conversations in another room.

He finished eating and stepped into the stirrup, feeling the muscular power of Gent beneath him as he settled into the cradle of his saddle. The creak of leather was reassuring in this alien land and as they moved back onto the road, John felt as rich as any man could be. He had a good horse, money in his pocket, gold in his saddlebags, and a friend waiting for him atop the mesa that jutted out from a mountain like the entrance to a shrine.

An hour later, a jackrabbit jumped in front of him and he heard the ominous rattle in a nearby bush. The rabbit bounded out of sight and the rattler went silent. A few moments later, he saw a man on horseback riding slowly toward him from the south. His senses perked up as if pricked by the spine of a Spanish bayonet, and his right hand dropped to the butt of his pistol.

There was something wrong with the rider. He was slumped in the saddle. The horse stepped out smartly, its hide sleek and black as velvet in the sun. An uncommon horse in such country, he thought, maybe four or five years old and tall, as graceful as a thoroughbred.

The road to the mine was close, just out of eyesight. But close.

John rode on, closing the distance between him and the lone rider.

When he got close enough, John called out.

"Ho, the rider. You all right?"

There was no answer, but he saw the man's arm rise and his right hand open.

He gripped the butt of his pistol and rode in close. Close enough to see the rider, a half-naked man gripping the reins and saddle horn with his left hand. His right arm now dangled by his side, scarlet with blood.

John knew he was looking at a Navajo warrior. The man's

leg was bleeding, too. The blood oozed out from under a
scab just below his knee, on the calf. His right shoulder was
wrapped with a blood-soaked bandanna that had loosened,
apparently, so that blood trickled down his arm.

"*Quién eres?*" he said in Spanish. *Who are you?*

"Coyote. *Yo soy Coyote.*"

John's pulse quickened. He reached out and tilted the
man's head so that he could see his face. Yes, it was Coyote.

"Do you know who I am?" John asked in Spanish.

"Yes. Do you have my knife?"

"I have it."

"I am dying. I want to take my knife with me."

"I will give it to you. Did you come to see me, Coyote?
How did you find me?"

"Yes. I see you from far away. And I talk to a man in a
wagon. He tell me you go to Tucson, come back this sun. I
come to give you warning. The white man Ollie. He is coming. He has many men. He comes to kill you, *Salvaje.*"

John felt his pulse pounding in his temple. Coyote had
used the Spanish word for Savage.

"Ollie told you this?"

"I ride the death trail, *Salvaje.* You were kind to me. You
did not kill me."

Coyote drew himself up and looked at John with sad
brown eyes that were misted with pain.

"How many men does Ollie bring with him?

"Four white men and Mano Rojo."

"When does Ollie come?"

"One more sun. He comes tomorrow."

John reached back and felt inside one of his saddlebags.
He found the knife, brought it out. Coyote's eyes widened
when he saw it.

"Can you come with me, Coyote?"

"No. Coyote die *muy pronto.*"

"I have medicines."

Coyote shook his head.

John handed him the knife. As Coyote grasped it with his

bloody right hand, John could almost feel the pain that ripped through the Navajo's body, could almost hear the silent scream that must be sounding in the man's brain.

Coyote slid the knife into the empty sheaf on his sash.

"Go with your god," Coyote said in Spanish.

"Where will you go?" John asked.

Coyote looked off into the distance.

"To the mountains," he said.

He did not say good-bye, but turned his horse toward the mountains, toward the west. As he rode off, John saw the army brand on the horse's hip. He watched him ride on, amazed at his courage, his fortitude. Coyote had a purpose, he knew, and he would get to the mountains and he would die all alone, close to the earth, under the sky.

The sun was falling in the western sky and soon John was blinded by the light and Coyote had disappeared.

He turned his horse and rode toward the road that would take him to the mine. His heart had lead in it, weighed heavy in his chest. He might not have been able to make Coyote well, but he knew he would have done it if Coyote had let him.

He would have made a friend out of an enemy if he could have.

If.

So Hobart was coming. And he had five men with him. One of them was Mano Rojo, the man who had killed Gale's husband.

As he topped the rise, he saw a wagon approaching. He recognized the wagon and the horses.

The two men spoke in Spanish. John asked him what he was called.

"I am called Romero. I take these dead ones to Tucson."

"The lieutenant?" John said.

"He is one, yes."

"You go alone?"

"The lady is on the mesa with your friend. I will return when the sun sets. There will be fighting, no?"

"Yes, there will be fighting?"

"This night?"

"No. Tomorrow."

"Did you see the Navajo who was hurt?"

"Yes, I saw him."

"He told me he was your friend. He said he was dying and wanted to say good-bye."

"He is dying. He said good-bye."

"I told him he would meet you."

"That was good to do."

"I would have killed him, but I knew he was dying. I could smell his death on him."

"There will be more dying tomorrow."

"Good. I am not afraid."

Romero smiled.

Perhaps he was brave, perhaps not. John couldn't tell. But he waved good-bye and continued on. For some reason he was glad Gale was with Ben up on the mesa. He thought maybe she was taking a shine to him, and perhaps Ben was interested in her. They were both about the same age, and both had lost much in the world.

But he was no matchmaker. Ben would have to fend for himself when it came to women.

When he reached the road, he saw men on horseback atop the mesa. He waved, wondering if they could see him from so far away.

He didn't want to be shot if they were men who worked for Gale, which he suspected they were.

One of the men waved back, while another turned his head toward the laboratory.

A few minutes later, John looked up and saw what looked to be Gale and Ben, and another man, all on foot.

All three waved at him and he smiled.

He felt good for a moment and waved back.

Yes, he felt good.

It almost felt like he was coming home.

And yet he knew, deep down, that he had no home.

And he never would have until Ollie Hobart was dead and he could put away his six-gun.

That accursed gun that was far too easy to draw and shoot.

And to kill.

28

JAKE WARD SEEMED A MERE SEMBLANCE OF HIS FORMER SELF. HE
had lost weight, for one thing. His clothes hung on him like
someone else's dirty laundry. He had not shaved in several
days and the wiry bristles of his beard could not conceal his
gaunt, emaciated face. He was covered with dust and reeked
of long sweaty hours in the saddle. His eyes were watery and
red-rimmed as if he had been rubbing them with sand or hot
chili peppers.

"You look like hell, Jake," John said as the two shook
hands.

"I been through it, sure enough," Jake said.

"Glad to see you, anyway. You run off from Ollie?"

"I sneaked off," Jake said, "and only got free by the skin
of my teeth. If most of the Navajos in Red Hand's band
hadn't been killed by the soldiers Ollie bushwhacked, he'd
have had me tracked and shot. Why he didn't send Red Hand
after me, I'll never know. Anyway, I never had a chance to
get Hobart, the bastard. He's as wily as a fox, and a thousand
times more dangerous."

Jake paused to get his breath, but it was plain that he had

a lot more on his mind than his escape from Ollie's band of outlaws.

"Look, John, I come here to warn you. Ollie knows about this mine up here and that you found gold. He's comin'. I don't know when, but you got to get out."

"I know he's coming," John said.

"You do? Then let's all hightail it out of here. He wants the gold, sure, but he wants you more than anything else. I tell you, Ollie's got blood in his eye. He means to put a bullet right square in your head or pump."

John sucked in a breath.

"That's good news," John said. "I want Ollie to come after me. Saves me the trouble of hunting him down in Mexico."

"You're plumb loco," Jake said.

"How do you know he's comin', John?" Ben asked.

John told him about Coyote.

"That injun told you that? And you trust a redskin?" Ben said.

"He was dying. Look, there's a lot to do. According to Coyote, Ollie and his men, as well as Red Hand, should be up here sometime tomorrow. Gale, we don't need all those men standing guard. Just one will do. On foot. You can relieve him every two hours. Ben and I will stand watch, too, if need be."

"My men will be glad to hear that," she said. "Shouldn't the guard be on horseback?"

"No. The guard should be sitting down. He can see far enough. But anyone down in the valley will find him hard to see if he's not sitting a horse."

"I understand," she said. "What you say makes good sense."

Gale picked her way through the piles of horse droppings and spoke to her men. All but one of the riders turned their horses. The last man dismounted and handed his reins to Gale. She came back to the lab, leading the riderless horse.

"Too bad we never built no stable up here," she said.

John nodded and turned to Ben.

"We need a place to hobble all the horses, Ben. Do you suppose you could scout a place on the other side of that mountain where the mine is?"

Ben stepped to one side of the lab and surveyed the terrain. There were smaller hills to the north, but the mountain was wide and rugged.

"There's a wide path down that side," Gale said. "Clarence sometimes tied up his horses in a little grassy swale. I don't know exactly where it is, but he told me about it. When he was up here for any length of time with several of our men, he said he kept the horses down there, out of the way."

"I'll ride down there and scout it," Ben said.

He started to go after his horse, then stopped.

"John, how many men has Ollie got with him?"

"Five or six, counting Mano Rojo."

"The numbers sound okay, but Ollie sure as hell ain't goin' to ride straight up the road right into our guns."

"No," John said, "I don't expect he will. I'll tell you my plan when you get back. See if you can't find that grassy place where we can quarter the horses."

"Yeah, sure," Ben said.

"Take Fidel with you," Gale said. "I think he's been there before."

Ben and Fidel rode off toward the far end of the tailings and disappeared over the side of the mesa. John walked to the edge of the tabletop and surveyed the road and the surrounding terrain. The guard, whose name was Benito Porres, spoke to him.

"What you look for?" he said.

"Places to hide men on both sides of that road."

"Like the *Indios*, eh?"

John nodded and walked the length of the escarpment from one side to the other.

He stood at the south end for several minutes, scanning the road, the rocky terrain that sloped away from the mesa. There were plenty of places where a man might conceal himself. But there were other considerations, as well. If they flanked the road, he would have to place rifles in close range to the road, but in such a way that those on the opposite flank would not be in the line of fire. He was not a military man, but he knew he had to think like one now. Their lives depended on his judgment. And he wanted to make sure that Ollie could not get away.

What would Ollie think when he came to this place?

He wasn't a stupid man. In fact, he was very smart and very clever. He was also very wary. He was like a wise old fox. If, when he rode up, he saw the slightest movement, heard a cough, or saw sunlight bouncing off a rifle barrel, he would elude any trap set for him.

Gale and Jake finally walked over and stood just behind John. They didn't speak or make a sound, for they surmised that he was thinking. John knew they were there, but he kept looking down at the south road and the road leading to the mesa and the mine.

There was another matter he had to work out, too. What would draw Ollie up the road? The man wasn't a fool. He would be thinking of ways to approach that were well away from the road. He would have a commanding view of the road, the mesa, and everything surrounding his path. And, too, he would have the eagle-eyed Mano Rojo with him, a Navajo warrior who could probably spot a sitting bird at a thousand yards.

Finally, John turned around and looked at Gale and Jake.

He gazed into Jake's eyes, then into Gale's.

"Two questions," he said.

They both looked at him in silence, waiting.

"Jake, are you a good shot?"

"I am. So I've been told."

"Gale, how good can your men shoot?"

"Not very good, I'm afraid," she said.

"So there's Jake, Ben, you, Gale, and me. Four good shots. We'll be facing five or six killers, men who seldom miss, probably.

"You worried, John?" Jake said.

"No. I don't want anyone here to get shot. I don't want any of you to die."

"That sounds like worry to me," Gale said.

"Just figuring the odds," John said.

"And?" Gale said before Jake could say the same thing.

"In our favor, maybe," John said.

"Look, John," Jake said, "I might not have gotten Ollie, but I want him as bad as you do. He killed my brother and I can't rest until he's paid for that. Just like you want him to pay for what he did to your family."

"I'm not questioning your courage, Jake.

"Then, what?"

"I'll tell you both. You have a right to know."

"Tell us," Gale said, brushing a strand of hair away from her eyes.

A breeze had sprung up as the sun settled on the far peaks to the west, throwing much of the land into pools of shadow and sunlight, gentling the valley below, painting it a soft purple, while the clouds blazed on the horizon, their underbellies gilded with copper and gold, their sides turning salmon and silver.

"I don't want Ollie to get away. I don't want to keep chasing him to the ends of the earth. I want him to die here, in this desolate but beautiful land. I want his blood to soak into the earth, right here, and bloom pretty flowers in the spring. I want all who ride with him to die, too, before the sun sets tomorrow night."

There was steel in his voice and his eyes had narrowed to black slits. His jaw had tightened until it appeared to have been sculpted with an ax. His face was dark, in shadow, yet he radiated an inner fire that smoldered like a mighty volcano.

"In the morning," John said, "I will reveal my plan to both of you, and to everyone. Just promise me this."

"What's that, John?

"That you will do my bidding without protest or question."

Jake and Gale both nodded. They could feel the heat within him, feel its banked rage just behind the iron door of a furnace.

29

JOHN BLEW WARM AIR ON HIS COLD FINGERS.

He shivered in the spiny chill that crept into his clothes, into his flesh, into his bones.

He lay in a shallow ditch, his body covered with brush he had cut and pulled over him.

He could see the faint outline of the road, just barely, and, out of the corners of both eyes, little pinpoints of light through the black tapestry of night. The moon was setting and Venus stood near the horizon, a watery vision of shimmery silver, the brightest object in the sky.

Above him, two hundred yards or so, he knew Ben was shivering in a similar hollow, his body covered with brush, and on the other side of the road, Jake lay in his trench, concealed under dirt and branches he and Ben had laid over him.

The three had not walked on the road, so they left no boot tracks for Mano Rojo to read. They had clambered off the mesa in the dark, making their way through rocks and cactus to their hideouts. After getting Jake positioned, John and Ben had climbed back up and come down on the opposite side of the road, stepping carefully to avoid dislodging rocks, leaving telltale signs of their passing for any keen eye to see.

A light breeze jostled the brush and John flexed his fingers to make sure his blood was circulating in them.

Dawn was at least a half hour or so away, and it seemed to him that the darkness was deepening, reluctant to give up its cloak to the light of day.

Gale had asked him if he wanted to eat before he had ventured out of the laboratory.

"No," he told her. "I always hunt on an empty stomach."

Gale and her sheepherders were not in the lab anymore. She and Romero were in the mine, near the entrance, huddled behind the wagon that they had pulled up in front of it the evening before. The other herders were behind the tailings, with orders not to show themselves unless some of Ollie's men rode up on the mesa.

John meant to see that this wouldn't happen.

He had given specific orders to Ben and Jake.

"Shoot their horses out from under them. I'll do the same. Then make sure you knock down Red Hand. I'll take on Ollie once he's on foot."

"What if he ain't?" Ben had asked.

"Then I'll get him on horseback."

Simple orders. A simple plan.

If it worked.

The smell of earth assailed John's nostrils. Dry, fragrant earth that might become his grave. He waited for the dawn, listening in the hushed night for any alien sound. Listening for the sound of horses approaching. Would he hear them? He put his ear to the ground and held it there, listening. He might hear them. Or he might not.

He watched the stars wink out, one by one, and then Venus vanish along with the pale ghost of the moon. A deep royal blue painted the sky and light appeared in the east like flowing cream, pale as his mother's bread pudding. Distant battens of clouds took on the hues of fishes, salmon and trout, their backs gray as dove wings. The threnodic sound of insects coming to life lent an insistent undertone to the sky's unfurling of banners as the sun rose, creeping up to gaze on the sleeping land like some giant flaming god.

The rider caught John by surprise. He had thought to see a half dozen, either riding in a pack or spread out or single file. But no, there was just one rider, turning onto the road that led to the mesa. A black silhouette on a horse of no color, coming out of the shadowy valley, picking its way slowly up the road, as unhurried as an aimless snail.

John's blood quickened. His temple throbbed with the furious beating of his heart. The sun crept higher, rising so slow he had not yet felt its heat.

Then John's stomach knotted as the rider drifted into the light. It was a lone Navajo, and he was leaning over, studying the tracks in the road. He made a guess who that Navajo was.

Mano Rojo. Red Hand.

"Don't shoot, you men," he said to himself. "Let him go." He prayed. He held his breath. A rock beneath him dug into his upper calf, yet he dared not move. Dared not make a sound. He let his breath out slow, through his nostrils so that no vapor would escape.

The Navajo rode up all the way to the overhanging lip of the tabletop. He halted for a few moments, turning his head one way, then the other.

John's breath caught in his throat, burned hot in his chest.

Red Hand turned his horse and raised one hand as if he were signaling someone. Then he rode slowly back down the road, not gazing downward this time, but looking on both sides of the road, staring at the solemn landscape with the keen eyes of a hunting hawk. As John would have expected him to do.

Don't move, Ben, he thought. *Jake, don't give it away.*

Moments later, John saw the other riders. There were five of them. In the lead was a man with the stature and build of Ollie Hobart, riding a steeldust gray. The horse's coat looked like moonbeams on a shadowy pond in the uncertain light of that tenuous dawn.

John drew in a deep, slow breath to steady himself. His rifle

lay beside him, ready to bring up when it was time. There
was a cartridge in the chamber. He rubbed his thumb on the
crosshatching of the hammer.

He waited.

Red Hand stopped and Hobart stopped. His men bunched
up behind him. They all carried rifles pointing skyward, the
butts resting on their thighs.

Red Hand spoke and made hand signs. He pointed up the
road, pointed to his ear, sailed the flat of his hand across an
invisible plane to show that the way was clear and all was
quiet.

The riders all came within range. Hobart drew his rifle
from its scabbard. John heard the sound of him jacking a
cartridge into the chamber. Red Hand left his rifle in its
scabbard, leading the way up the road.

John measured the distance with his gaze, noted the
progress of the horses. Ben and Jake were not supposed to
shoot until they heard the sound of his rifle. He hoped they
held to that order.

John eased his rifle up to his shoulder. He placed the barrel gently on a rock and took aim at the steeldust gray. He
calculated the horse's speed and eased the barrel over, waiting for Hobart's horse to come into his sights.

John gave the trigger of his Winchester a slight squeeze,
depressing it so that the mechanism would not be heard. He
thumbed back the hammer and there was no sound. He released the trigger. Finally, when Hobart was directly opposite, John started his slow steady swing. He held his breath,
led the horse a fraction of an inch, kept the barrel moving,
took a breath, held it, and squeezed the trigger. He was aiming for the steeldust's heart.

The thunder in his ears deafened him momentarily as the
rifle bucked against his shoulder, spat out smoke and sparks,
the deadly projectile. He saw the horse stagger and fall to its
right side.

"Damn," Hobart yelled as his horse collapsed beneath
him. His rifle went flying out of his hands and clattered some
yards away as it struck a pile of rocks.

Then Ben and Jake opened up and horses began tumbling like dominoes on a table. Men screamed and men yelled. Hobart flung himself to the side of the road, flattened like a cat on a tree limb. John levered another cartridge into the chamber. The ejected shell clanged on a rock. He picked out a running man, led him, squeezed the trigger, and saw the man fling up his arms and go down in a heap. Other men dashed back and forth. Ben's rifle accounted for one, Jake's another.

Red Hand was still on horseback. John saw him race up the hill. He tried to draw a bead on him and before he could fire, the Navajo's horse clambered up on the mesa and disappeared.

John's heart stuck in his throat.

He heard more firing from both Ben's rifle and Jake's.

Where was Hobart?

John couldn't see him.

The guns went quiet and there was a long silence.

John laid his rifle aside and rose from his hiding place and started walking toward the road. His right hand rested on the butt of his pistol.

"Hobart," he called.

There was a loud grunt and Hobart stood up. His right hand was cocked like a frozen bird above his pistol.

"That you, Savage?" Hobart said.

"Looks like it's just you and me, Ollie," John said. "Isn't that the way you wanted it?"

"Damned right, Savage. You been breathin' my air too long."

"Didn't Red Hand tell you, Ollie?"

"Tell me what?" Hobart snarled his words. The two men were very close, within ten paces of each other. Hobart stood his ground, while John took one more step and then stopped.

"That this is the end of the road for you."

"Why, you sonofa . . ."

That was as far as Hobart got. His hand dove for his pistol as he went into a fighting crouch.

John stood straight, his right hand like magic as it jerked

his pistol from its holster. His thumb pulled the hammer back to full cock and when the pistol came level, a split second before Hobart could aim his own, John squeezed the trigger, the hair trigger that took just a touch, and his pistol barked and spat out lead and fire and brimstone from waist high.

In the distance, John heard the sharp report of a rifle. It sounded as if it came from somewhere near the mine.

He saw a flower, a crimson flower, blossom on Hobart's chest. Blood spouted from a hole right where his heart should have been. Hobart gagged and choked, pitched forward. His fingers turned limp as boiled noodles and his pistol fell to the road with a thud.

John walked over to him, stood over the dying man.

"End of the road, Hobart," John said softly.

Hobart's eyes glazed over with the icy frost of death and then fixed on the blue sky above him. A last gasp escaped his lips and his body convulsed into a rigid contorted corpse.

Ben and Jake approached cautiously, their rifles ranging from one fallen man to another.

"They're all dead," John said.

"You get Hobart?" Ben asked.

"There he lies, Ben. See for yourself."

And the three men walked toward the mine.

RED HAND LAY SPRAWLED ON THE GROUND THIRTY YARDS FROM the mine entrance.

"You can come out now, Gale," John called. "All of you can come out."

Men rose from behind the tailings. Gale and Romero emerged from the mine, walked around the parked wagon.

"I got the bastard," Gale said. "I got the bastard what killed Clarence."

"You sure did," Ben said, and the pride in his voice was as strong as Gale's had been.

"Did you get Hobart?" Gale asked.

"He sure did," Ben said. "Right in his black heart."

"I guess that pistol knew what to do," Gale said, looking at John.

John looked down. He still had the Colt in his hand. The sun glinted off the silver, off the words etched there so long ago by his father.

"I guess it knew, and I guess it had reason to do what it did."

He smiled, thinking of the legend inscribed on the barrel.
No me saques sin razón, ni me guardes sin honor.